Star of Danger

Star of Danger

Jane Whitbread Levin

Harcourt, Brace & World, Inc.
New York

Contents

Historical Note

On October 1, 1943, the eve of the Jewish New Year, the German Government of Occupation in Denmark during World War II ordered the arrest of all Jews in Denmark. At that time Denmark's Jewish population was estimated at eight thousand, including a few hundred Germans who had escaped from Nazi persecution in their homeland.

Among this small group was Karl Friedberg. Four years before, when he was fourteen, he had left his family in Düsseldorf on the Rhine and set out in hope of freedom. This is his story.

Star of Danger

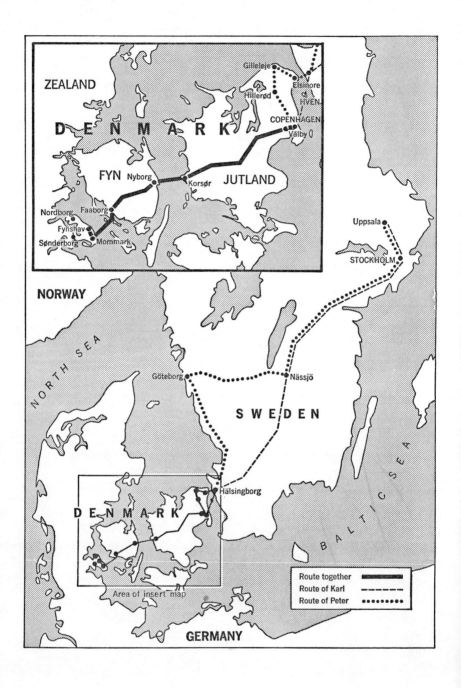

✿ 1 ✿

Karl

Karl grew up in the industrial city of Düsseldorf, Germany. He lived in a flat over a butcher shop on a cobblestoned street above the Rhine with his father, mother, and older brother, Richard.

His father, a skilled steel worker, was stern and strict, but fair and reasonable. His mother kept the family's small apartment perfumed with the mingled smells of baking, of the wild flowers she brought home from walks in the neighboring woods, and of lemon oil, with which she made their simple furniture gleam. She had hot chocolate ready when the boys brought their friends home from skating in the winter, and lemonade and cookies on the top shelf of the refrigerator when they came in from play, overheated and lazy, on summer afternoons.

Karl was a perfectly ordinary thirteen-year-old. But the amount of activity he could cram into each of his days was extraordinary even for thirteen. In the summer he was up with the sun and out of the house before the rest of the family had stirred. He would bounce out of bed and into his shorts and T-shirt. He would grab up his treasured track shoes, earned by polishing brass for his mother and running errands for the butcher downstairs, and tiptoe through the flat. Outside, he would shut the door silently, light on the top step long enough to slip into his shoes, then spring into action. On the ridge above their house, he would meet a friend and start a two-mile jog out of town. Sometimes on the way home they would stop to tease a treeful of starlings with pebbles or pick daisies and buttercups for the breakfast table. Sometimes they would race in earnest—timing themselves with a stop watch and carefully noting their records in the notebook each kept in his hip pocket.

When Karl got back, the family would be at breakfast. His father would tell him to be sure and wash thoroughly and complain about all the work he made for his mother with his running clothes and his cycling clothes and his school shirts. But his mother would beam at the flowers he'd brought and say: "One egg or two, Karl?"

And every day he would say: "You know I don't like eggs, Momma," as if the joke were fresh. Five minutes later—washed and dressed—he would down his bun and bitter milky coffee, grab his books and lunch bag, kiss his mother good-by, and run to catch up with his father and brother who had already started down the stairs to the street.

At the bottom of the hill, Richard and their father

took the bus toward the city. All the way to the inter-
section, where he turned off the river road to get to
school, Karl would try to keep up with their bus on his
bike. At the turn, or pedaling toward him, he would find
one of his friends. The boys would race ahead, talking
about homework, reciting formulae or verb endings to
each other, or laying plans for the day. At some point one
would fall silent, crouch over his racer-style handlebars
like a professional, and begin pedaling in earnest. The
other would fall in, and they would ride on, streaking
into the schoolyard and braking to a quick stop. Leaving
their bikes in the racks outside the entrance, they would
hurry to get to their seats before the bell.

After school they might wheel their bikes and walk
part way with the girls whose school was on the same
road. But usually more pressing business claimed them.
Karl had to get home to hurry through his chores and
his work at the butcher's so that he would be free for
his own activities. There was band practice. There was
practice for speed on their bikes. There was the new
kitchen cabinet he was making for his mother for Christmas. And finally there was homework, which he at-
tacked as energetically as he did his drums.

After supper, the door of their room shut, Karl and
his brother worked side by side at matching desks they
had built together. Richard hardly looked up from his
work. Karl studied by fits and starts. He worked so fast
at his math that his pencil scarcely seemed to have
time to mark the page before he was finished. Then he
would take one of the darts lying on the desk and start
aiming at the target nailed to the back of the bedroom

door. After a game alone he couldn't resist coaxing Richard to join. Usually he succeeded. Five minutes later both boys would get back to work until Karl interrupted again to ask Richard to look over his mechanical drawing work or try him on spelling or English vocabulary.

There were intermissions, too, for chats with their father, snacks from the kitchen, or extra drum practice.

Even after Richard had gone to bed, Karl parted slowly with the day. He would sink into his father's chair and look at the paper, or shine his shoes, or oil his track shoes before he finally climbed into the bunk bed above his brother's and settled down for the night.

After his thirteenth birthday party, he said to his father and mother: "Maybe thirteen is an unlucky number, but it's been my best year so far."

He had won the 100-meter race at the city stadium, which meant he would compete for a place in the national track finals the next summer.

He had been accepted at the trade school he hoped for. And, most important, he had a real job. Hermann Grossbart, who owned the cabinet-making shop at the foot of their hill, had asked him to be his apprentice.

But hardly a month later, hurrying home to work with Mr. Grossbart as usual, Karl noticed smoke ahead. As he drew closer, he saw a big bonfire in the middle of the street. It was Mr. Grossbart's furniture—the sideboard they were to deliver that very day and the chairs they were still working on, to go with it. The store itself was wrecked. The plate glass window was

in shards all over the sidewalk. The fixtures were pulled
out of the ceiling.

He threw his bike down and ran to save some of the
chairs and tables that the fire had not reached. Before
he could pull out a stick of molding, an angry voice
shouted: "Watch out, kid, you might get burned." When
he saw that it was only one of the familiar hangers-on
at the beer hall, he waved in friendly fashion and turned
back to saving the furniture. He felt a hand on his arm
and a painful wrench. The fellow had grabbed him. He
was holding a pistol in Karl's face. "Don't you understand the Führer's orders? Get out of here—before we
find out how long you'd take to roast."

Karl suppressed a yell of terror and pain. There was
no one on the deserted street to help. The man let go.
Karl ran for his bike and got away as fast as he could
down the river road. His mother was not at the door to
meet him when he got home. She wasn't in the living
room. She didn't answer when he called. In the kitchen
the butter and sugar for a cake were in the mixing
bowl. The eggs were ready beside it. Still no answer. He
looked in the bedroom to see if her coat was there. She
was lying on the bed. When he came in, she struggled
to her feet and put her arms around him, trying not to
cry.

"Karl," she said, "the Nazis have come. Have you
seen your father? He's looking for you."

All over the city, she told him, the homes of Jews had
been searched. Two Brownshirts had broken into their
apartment, ransacked the drawers and closets, taken
the beautiful Dresden china clock that had belonged to

his great grandmother, emptied the silver into their pockets, and stormed out. The roar of their motorcycles had hardly died before Mr. Friedberg ran up the stairs. When he found the boys were still out, he left at once to find them, warning his wife to keep them at home if they got back before he did.

During the years of Hitler's rise to power, the Friedbergs had watched the Nazi uniforms multiply, had smarted under the insults of neighbors who had once been friends, and had heard the rasping voice of the Führer and the chilling roar from the crowds of "Heil, Hitler," with growing fear. Now their suspicions were confirmed.

That day Karl's employer, Mr. Grossbart, disappeared. That day Karl was barred from classes at the trade school. That day his father lost his job, and his brother, who had started work as a pharmacist a few short weeks before, was finished. But the Friedbergs were lucky. They were still safe together. Mr. Friedberg promised that he would get exit permits soon. Uncle Franz was sure his American friend would set them up in the Berkshires—part of New England very much like their Rhineland.

Months passed. Each evening at supper there was the inevitable question they all tried not to ask: "Did you hear anything, today, Father?"

And the quiet, unchanging answer: "Not today. It takes time."

Friends got their permits and left. Relatives disappeared without saying good-by. One night Mr. Friedberg said: "Uncle Franz says his friend can help no more. We must have money."

Karl's father continued making his daily visits to the emigration department and writing his daily letters to people distantly related by marriage several generations back, and to others in America with whom the connection was even more remote, but the boys had lost hope. They began to make plans of their own. Whichever one got a chance to go, they agreed, would take it with no apologies and no regrets. Once outside Germany, he would try to help the rest of the family.

At Hebrew school, where Karl was trying to continue the studies that he had been cut off from at the trade school, the library was stacked with literature from Jewish organizations all over the world. He wrote to them all—in Europe, Palestine, the United States. The replies were disheartening. "We are sorry, but we have been unsuccessful in securing exit permits for prospective students at our institute."

"We regret that our organization is already overextended and can supply no further funds."

"Please keep in touch with us."

"We do not accept children unless accompanied by a parent. If your father will apply for an exit permit for his family . . ."

Finally, however, diligence paid off. A letter came from a rabbi in the United States who had heard of his appeal from the head of one of the organizations to which Karl had written.

The man told him of a camp near Hanover, Germany, belonging to an international organization that trained boys for farm work in Palestine.

"You are too young," his letter said, "but you show the courage, strength, and leadership that our people need so badly. I have written my friend at the camp, and I am sure that if he has been spared, you will hear from him."

Karl would have set out for the camp on foot at once, but no name, no address, nothing more was in the letter. For weeks he and his brother waited for the mailman's visit each day. They had almost forgotten the rabbi's promise when a letter finally came. Karl was home alone. He started to open it, then decided to wait for Richard.

At dusk his brother came home lugging a bag full of coal he had scavenged along the tracks in the freight yard. Karl went downstairs to meet him. The letter was from the camp, urging him to come at once.

The escape he had almost stopped hoping for was now in sight, but the elation Karl had anticipated failed to materialize. The thought of leaving his mother and father and Richard made him fearful. More than once his brother had to remind him of their pact to keep Karl from backing out and staying in Düsseldorf.

In the end, however, he did follow the instructions in the letter. The following morning he left for the camp in Hanover, a day's journey away. Six weeks later, he had completed his preliminary training for agricultural work and was on his way to Denmark, where he was to stay, getting further practical experience, until he could be transported to Palestine. In less than a year his language had changed from German to Danish; his home from the apartment in Düsseldorf to a three-hundred-year-old North Jutland farmhouse of timbered stucco; his trade from cabinetmaker to farm hand.

From their meeting on the first day of camp at Hanover, Peter Wolf was Karl's friend, companion, and substitute for the family left behind. Peter came from Hamburg and before 1938 (when the persecution of the Jews exploded) had never dreamed of being anything but a banker like his father. The nearest thing to manual labor he had ever known was on the playing fields at school.

One of the boys' strongest bonds had been their mutual distaste for farming. But the Nordbys in Jutland, where they went to wait their turn for passage to Palestine, made them forget the hard work and long hours in the fields and barns. After the first days they stopped complaining, even to each other.

No matter how tired everyone was by Saturday, they all hurried through the afternoon chores and the last milking to get bathed and dressed for an evening of fun. If there wasn't a family party to go to, there were country celebrations in honor of May day or the budding of the beech trees or midsummer night, or there was a county fair.

Before their second harvest in Denmark, Peter and Karl had become so firmly established in their neighborhood that they were hardly distinguishable from their Danish fellows. If they had not always had an ear cocked for news from home and word to proceed to Palestine, they would have become almost Danish, in fact

almost Nordbys. But no word came. At the end of the
summer of 1942, when they had still heard nothing, Mr.
Nordby decided to make them true Danes. The first step
was a term at Folk High School, where all the Nordbys
had gone.

"I'm not going to read a big sermon about what
Folk High School means to us. You go and come back
and tell us what you think," he said.

"It's not a regular school. There are no tests or marks
or prizes. The teachers are there to help you learn whatever they can teach you about your work and our country. There'll be boys and girls your age from factories
and shipyards and farms. For five months you'll learn
just what *you* want to learn."

The following Sunday they piled into the back of the
farm truck with their small rucksacks and the five
Nordby children and bounced over the farm road to the
north-south route that would take them to the byroad to
Fynshav—right above the German border.

Ten minutes after they had reached the highway, a
truck stopped at their signal. The boys threw their
belongings in with the mail and got into the seat beside
the driver. The car moved off again, and the boys waved
to the Norstad family until they were out of sight.

They never went back to Jutland. Halfway through
the term Peter was taken to the hospital, unable to walk
for the sudden pain in his thigh. The doctors diagnosed
a rare bone disease from which recovery is slow and un-
certain. By summer Peter was well enough to leave the
hospital, but the doctors wanted him nearby so that they
could watch him for a while. Friends of the Nordbys in

Nordborg welcomed Peter into their family, where he could help the children with schoolwork in return for board and room. The headmaster's family at the Folk School invited Karl to stay with them. And Mr. Troner, the headmaster, got him work with a cabinetmaker in Sønderborg. Karl tried to repay them in part by working around the school and helping with the Troner children.

✿ 2 ✿

The Letter

The Danish Folk High School, nestled against the whisper of a hill above the village of Fynshav and the blue waters of Lille Baelt, looked comfortable and ready for the night. It was late September, 1943, and the fall term had not begun. In the big school dining room, only a few teachers and Karl Friedberg were at supper with the headmaster's family at the round table nearest the living room.

It was unnaturally quiet. Instead of the animated conversation of one hundred and eighty students and the clatter of silver and dishes, there was only the gentle hum of voices at the Troners' table, punctuated by the staccato of the village girls' heels as they went back and forth serving.

Karl sat at one end of the table with Mrs. Troner and the three Troner children. The girls were talking to their mother about the pattern and colors for the table mats she had promised to help them weave before school started. But Timmy Troner was deep in conversation with Karl about a sailing race two days away.

"Please, Karl," he begged, "don't make me be captain. We're sure to lose."

Karl laughed. "It's not *that* important, Tim. Suppose we *do* lose. Don't you think it would be nice for someone else to see what it's like to win?"

"Next time? Please, Karl, next time?"

"No next time. You've got to learn to be captain."

"Suppose I got sick or something?"

"You get sick? Impossible."

"I promise I'll take over next week, Karl."

"*I* promise you'll do it Saturday. Come on. Winning's not everything, Tim. Think of the excitement of having the helm to yourself. Matter of fact, we have a good chance. You should be quicker going about than I am. You're so light. That makes a big difference on tacking."

Timmy made a last plea. "You know the currents better. I won't know which way to go."

Karl agreed to navigate and said they'd have to plan the strategy for the race after they found out what the course for the day would be and what kind of breeze they had.

The girls had cleared the table. Now they brought in sugar, cream as thick as whipped butter, and plates piled high with brown-edged cookies. The room was full of the appetizing perfume of butter, vanilla, and freshly brewed coffee. Mrs. Troner began to pour, and Karl passed the cups. There was a ring at the front door, and a minute later Niels Holman, the postman, came in with the regular evening mail.

Mrs. Troner greeted him. Then Mr. Troner began his usual joking. "Aren't you a little late, Niels? I'm afraid we've finished off dessert." Niels's fondness for sweets was legendary. "Karl, maybe you can find him some coffee, anyway. Have some, Niels?"

"Why not," the postman replied, "while I wait for your answer to this."

He handed a special delivery letter to Mr. Troner and put the rest of the school mail down beside his plate.

Karl took the empty coffee pot to the kitchen to be filled.

Mr. Troner picked up the letter. "Copenhagen— from Edlund, eh? He must want a loan. I've never known that fellow to waste vacation time writing to me."

Edlund, a young history teacher who helped with sports, was a favorite of the children's. "What does he say? When is he coming back?" they asked at once. Mr. Troner didn't seem to hear. When he had finished the letter, he folded it slowly and carefully slipped it back into its envelope. Then he got up from the table. There was something in his manner that discouraged the children from asking him again.

"Come on, Niels," he said to the postman, who was talking and joking with the others at the table. "Let's go to my study. I'll give you the answer there where I have pen and paper. Karl, will you bring the coffee when it's ready?"

"And see if you can't find a few crumbs of cake to go

with it," Niels called over his shoulder. They walked out together.

One of the girls came in with the coffee and handed the tray to Karl.

Karl took a quick look. "Come on, Herta," he said. "Three cookies won't be enough for Niels. Where are you hiding them?"

At this the children got up with their plates and slid their own cookies onto Karl's tray.

In the general laughter Herta said: "I'll bring more for everyone before Karl gets back." And she hurried off to the kitchen.

"I'll beat you back," Karl called after her. He swung the tray up on his shoulder, balancing it in such perilous fashion that the children shrieked with mock terror as he sailed out of the dining room. When he put the tray down on the headmaster's battered desk, Mr. Troner looked up with his usual open smile and motioned him to the chair next to him. Karl poured the coffee and put the plate of cookies between the two men. Niels got up and shut the door.

"The letter is about you, Karl," Mr. Troner began in his quiet voice.

The headmaster went on. "We should have prepared you, but it's too late now. We have been warned by reliable friends that all the Jews in Denmark will be arrested any day. You must disappear at once."

Karl looked stunned. There was nothing to say. The shock was just as sudden as it had been the first time. The German occupation troops had been in Denmark for three years—trying to make friends, begging to be liked, and ignoring the snubs of the Danes, who looked right through them and pretended not to understand what they said. What had changed?

The lighthearted, easygoing Niels, deadly earnest now, explained the situation as briefly as he could.

The tables had turned. Hitler's pet canary—as Denmark had been nicknamed—was to be paid back for her ingratitude. Of all the lands occupied by the Nazis, she alone had been well treated. Maybe it was because of her blue-eyed, freckled, blond boys and girls? Or perhaps it was because of a more practical consideration: Germany needed a land route to bring in Sweden's iron and coal for her war machine. Germany needed the cheese, butter, and bacon Danish farms could supply. It would be risky to stir up the historic hostility of Danes for Germans. The Danes were allowed to run their own government, police their own people, and the King continued to head the state and live in his palace.

But the Danes hadn't cooperated with the Germans. The trains and truckloads of Swedish goods traveling through Jutland from Sweden kept being blown up. The bridges crumbled under the trains carrying the freight of war. The shipyards proved slower and slower. Finally, a few months before, strikes had broken out in the shipyards of Copenhagen. Hitler had ordered reprisals. And as usual, when the Nazis got tough, the Jews were the first scapegoats.

"You couldn't be in a more vulnerable spot than you are here," Niels said urgently. "You are the only Jew in miles. Anyone who has ever heard of the Folk School knows you're with us. You've gotten away once. The Nazis are not likely to let a boy with a German accent slip through their fingers twice."

Then it was Mr. Troner's turn. "This would be a poor place to hide under any circumstances. The Folk Schools are the most Danish thing in Denmark. We're prime suspects. We haven't had much trouble here, and we're out of the way, but at this point that might be just one more reason to keep an eye on us. It's too easy for people to hide here."

"They've been watching us for some time, now," Niels said. "We know it."

We. Karl wondered at that. After all, the postman wasn't part of the school. Was there another "We"— that Mr. Troner belonged to, too? "You and Mr. Troner aren't running. I'll stay with you. Why am I different?"

"Because you're the target for today. You know where the border is. We're not ten miles from Germany. Many of the villagers have parents or brothers there. There are people in town, even in this school, whom we can't be sure of. You have to go—as much for our safety as for your own. That's all we can tell you tonight. But remember, we have help. You will not be alone."

Karl's voice was as calm and clear as usual. "I won't leave without Peter. I'll have to get him."

Niels spoke again. "Don't worry about Peter. He's being taken care of. Go on as usual now. You've been away from the table too long already."

Karl was firm. "I won't go without Peter," he repeated.

Mr. Troner intervened. "I understand. You shouldn't.

But don't waste time. You'll have to go for him alone. It's too late for us to help."

The men hurried with the last of their coffee and cookies. Mr. Troner kept on talking. "We don't want to know where you're going. Just vanish. Stay away, hidden during the day. At night you can use the museum. When we find out what you're to do next, we'll leave you a note under the egg-shaped limestone rock I pointed out when we were in the beech woods beyond the south meadow last week. Remember?"

Karl nodded.

Mr. Troner stood up and embraced him. "Try to be patient."

Karl picked up the tray and left. He couldn't trust himself to look at the men or even say the word "good-by."

But when he went to the dining room, he kicked open the swinging door as if nothing had happened and swept through to the kitchen. The dining room was empty. When he came back to the table, only Timmy was waiting. Tim passed the cookie plate. "Have a special treat on me."

They picked up their discussion of the race where they had left it. When Tim's mother came to call her son for bed, Karl was explaining a trick with the jib sheet that would allow them to make a turn almost without slowing up. He had begun to explain the danger of pinching too close to the wind.

"Aw, Mom," Tim complained. "This is important. I'm learning a lot."

But that night Karl sided with Mrs. Troner. "Go on, Tim. We may not have school tomorrow, but you do."

They got up and walked out into the hall together. After Tim had said good night and gone to his room, Mrs. Troner spoke in typical motherly fashion. "You'd better take your jacket, Karl. The evenings are quite cold now."

Then in quite a different tone, almost in a whisper, she went on hurriedly "Understand me clearly. Don't show yourself by day. I'll leave that little cellar door behind the shrubbery unlocked. There'll be food under the workbench. The museum should be safe at night. I won't say good-by. This won't last much longer. The Nazis will be finished soon, the way things are going. Come back, Karl. We'll be waiting." And then she was gone.

He took the stairs two at a time as he always did and dashed to his room. He didn't need a light. He could find his jacket on the familiar hook just by reaching. He slipped it on and started to go. At the door he turned back to his desk for the picture of his family. He had it in his hand. Then he put it back. It was superstitious, he knew, but he hoped leaving it there would help bring him back.

Outside, he took his bike from the rack. Then he paused. He hadn't an idea in his head about what to do next, but he couldn't stand there to make his plans.

With one foot on the pedal, he pushed off, swung his other leg over the bike, and pedaled hard and sure up the drive just as usual. At the road, four hundred yards ahead, he turned left, away from town. Pushing himself, he kept on over the top of the hill until he was certain that he could no longer be seen from school. Then he stopped and, crouching low, retraced his steps until he was close to the peasant cottage that Mrs. Troner had made into a little museum of folk arts. He hid his bike in the high grass behind the low-lying building and dropped down against the wall to think.

Ten minutes later he was off on his roundabout way over the back roads and cow paths, which he knew well from his walks with the children, to get Peter. He hoped he would find him asleep in the Larsens' farmhouse, which was near Nordborg, twelve miles up the island of Als.

☼ 3 ☼

Under Cover

The stars were dazzling in the black clear night. The only sounds along the deserted farm roads were the crunch of his bicycle tires in the sand and the keening of mourning doves in the groves of beech or oak that broke the fields.

Karl traveled to the edge of the Larsen farm where Peter lived without seeing a soul. Only the light from the German headquarters in the former village store and post office directly across the road from the farmhouse reminded him that his mission was extraordinary.

He hid in the bushes at the main pasture gate to see that no one was moving. Then bending low over his bike, he started across the open space to the barn. A dog began to growl. It was too late to turn back. He plunged on as fast as he could. By now the farmer's collie was barking as if to raise the dead.

Karl saw someone getting up behind the window

across the road. He slid the last few yards to cover behind the barn. The barking continued. In the headquarters the door opened. A man came out. Against the light Karl could see him looking first one way, then the other. Another door opened. Then he heard Mr. Larsen calling the dog to come in. The barking stopped.

The soldier across the road went back inside. The door shut behind him. Karl saw him sit down again opposite his companion.

The cry of the mourning dove, clear, piercing, ineffably soulful, was the single sound in the lonely night. Karl waited. Farmers don't call in their watchdogs when they bark, he thought. They investigate. Did that mean the Larsens expected him? Then Niels's words came back: "There are people we can't be sure of." Karl could not be sure.

He stayed where he was. In a little while the men at the window across the road got up. The door opened again. Two soldiers came out and stood in front of the house, walking up and down, looking up at the sky, talking and smoking. After what seemed forever, the door closed again behind them. The bolt clicked shut in the lock. One of the men sat down alone. His head was bent over. He must have been reading or writing a letter home. He looked up not at all. The rest of the lights in the house went out. The road was quiet.

In a silent dash Karl ran for the farmhouse, then crept along the far side. At the corner of the front porch, he stopped behind a clump of bushes to get his breath. From here he could peer out to see what was going on across the road. The guard's position had not changed.

Now the only risk was the dog. It was a risk he had to take. He lifted himself from the porch railing to the roof. His heart pounded so that it was hard to breathe. He had to stand up. For the second that it took to cross the roof and flatten himself under Peter's window, he was perfectly silhouetted against the whitewashed wall of the house. He made it successfully. There was still nothing stirring across the road. The dog was quiet. Cautiously he lifted his head to call Peter through the open window.

The bed was empty. There were not even any clothes lying around. His friend was gone.

Karl wasted no time getting back on the ground. There was only one thing to do: get back to home territory before daylight. If there was any way to find Peter, it would be through the message center Mr. Troner had established in the beech woods.

There was no traffic at all on the highway this late at night. The road was straight and flat all the way. He would hear an approaching car in plenty of time to find cover. Unless someone were lying in wait for him, he'd be perfectly safe on the main route.

He circled down through the fields for about a mile below the headquarters building and came out on the path through the south pasture. Once on the highway, he rode close to the side so the hedgerows that bordered the fields would give him cover.

A mile from school he left the road again, circling below the village close to the water's edge.

The area was totally deserted this time of year. Half a dozen summer cottages dotted the fields. Their win-

Star of Danger

dows were boarded; their doors were locked. Their keys had been turned in to the local postmaster, and the owners had long since departed for their winter's work in Copenhagen. In the moonless night the houses looked black and lonely. They cast no shadows. Nothing about them stirred or made a sound. And yet, all at once the night was full of foreboding. What might not be concealed behind the barred doors and shuttered windows?

Karl pulled his bike into the grass to wait until he was calmer. But his panic, like a child's sudden fear of the dark, would not go away. From the house on the left a figure emerged. Karl buried his head in helpless anticipation of the end and waited, paralyzed. There was no sound. Finally he looked up. The figure was still emerging from the corner of the house. It was a lilac bush. Plainly it could never have been anything else.

He almost laughed with relief. He got back on his bicycle and rode on along the shoreline beyond the last farm before the beech woods. Then, well away from the house and barns, he turned up to the woods, where he had decided to hide during the day. He concealed his bicycle among some bushes under the trees and added a camouflage of fallen leaves for good measure.

With a mixture of hope and dread, he ran into the heart of the grove to the stone where the messages were to be. A note was there. He stuffed it into his pocket and looked for a tree trunk broad enough to hide him from the road on the other side of the woods.

When he was settled against the tree, he took the paper out to read the message. Then he realized he had no matches, no light of any kind. He would have to wait till dawn to find out what was happening.

The disappointment drained his last bit of courage. He knew he could easily make it to the door in the cellar and to the workbench where he would find food, and matches, too. But the quarter of a mile between him and school seemed endless.

He fell into a fitful sleep, waking every few minutes, sure that he had missed his rendezvous or lost his way. Each time he wakened, he tried to read the message. Before he could see mist rising off the bay in the early light of a new day, he managed to decipher it: "Your paths have crossed in the night. Friends will meet again. Wait."

He fell into a deep sleep now. When he woke up again, the day was well along. He had been awakened by a strange bird, a noisy bird, an unfamiliar bird that was scolding an unseen culprit. At first it seemed to be part of the confusion of a dream. Then Karl realized that the sound was real—if not the sound of a real bird. Over near the stone he saw Timmy.

Whatever creature Timmy was presuming to address in the branches high above him, he was using a bird song Karl had never heard and one invented, he suspected, simply to attract attention. Karl ducked down and waited. The calls and chatter stopped. He looked up to see Timmy's retreating back as he ran out into the fields and out of sight. He must have left a note.

Karl had to control the impulse to hurry over to the stone at once to get the message. He must wait until just before sundown. Then the traffic on the highway border-

ing the woods almost stopped. People who had been to
Sønderborg during the day to work or shop had returned
home for the evening meal. The farmers had left the
fields to their cattle for the night. It would be almost
dusk.

Before it got too dark to see, Karl crept out to pick
up Timmy's note. "Museum closed. Don't try it. Sailing
tomorrow as usual. Regular time and place."

☀ 4 ☀
The Rendezvous

What did it mean?

Wide awake now, with nothing to do but think, Karl faced the fact that for days or weeks, or perhaps months, he would be running from pursuers he would not know to equally mysterious rescuers. From one day to another, he would not know what his next move would be or where it would lead. At that moment, alone in the semidarkness, he would have welcomed a knife to whittle with, an apple to munch on—anything to distract him from his fears.

When he was reasonably sure that supper at school would be over and all the kitchen helpers gone, he made his way across the road into the orchards on the south side of school land. The main building was totally dark. He hurried along on the far side of the shrubbery that bordered the lawn, crossed the twenty yards of grass,

39

and ducked behind the evergreens that screened the foundation. The knob of the little cellar door was in his hand. Once inside, he shut the door behind him and relaxed against it, trying to get his breath while his eyes got used to the dark.

Slowly he felt his way to the workbench. On the shelf below he found chicken, tomatoes, apples, bread, and cake. Beside the plate was a pitcher of milk. What he couldn't eat he stuffed into his pockets.

There were matches, too. By striking one at a time, he got enough light to find the most useful tools he could conceal in his clothes—and set out again into the night.

The fields and village were quiet. Once more it seemed hard to believe that a search was on. Except for the loneliness, he would have felt almost carefree. He started back to the woods. Halfway through the orchard he hesitated. Instead of going on to the road, he turned sharply down toward the water.

The sky was starless, and there was dampness in the air. If there was rain, he would be completely unprotected in the beech woods. In the summer cottages, he would be dry, and besides, from there to the next day's rendezvous with Timmy on the far side of the village, the route would be half as long and half as dangerous. He could follow the water, keeping completely out of sight from the land side, then double back beyond the village to the fork where they were to meet.

He decided on the cottage that belonged to Niels Bohr. It was rumored that the famous physicist had chosen exile from his country in order to help the Allies against the Nazis. Besides, Bohr was a Jew. Certainly he would welcome Karl tonight if he could.

The house—forty yards below a dirt road leading to a large farm and a good quarter of a mile from the nearest dwelling—was well located. Anyone coming from the village to look for him would have to approach down a little hill. If Karl kept a sharp lookout, he could spot them and escape along the shore before they could reach the house.

After scouting the premises carefully, he unshuttered a shore-side window, lifted the lock with a file, opened the casements, and hoisted himself up and in, locking the shutters behind him at once.

The thick walls and boarded doors and windows made him feel safe and snug. Even so, he was afraid to light a match, but despite the darkness he got his bearings. There was a fairly large living room with a fireplace on the inside wall. Two small bedrooms opened off of it on one side, and a small kitchen and a storage room were on the other. The furniture seemed sparse and simple—probably old peasant-made chairs and tables. The one big round table must have been used both for dining and for work. There were low rope beds. He finally found the mattresses for them hanging from the ceiling, put there, probably, to keep out dampness and nesting field mice. He untied a mattress and got it down with little trouble and was asleep almost as soon as he had put it on a bed.

In the morning, light filtered through the shutters, providing him with a better view of his accommodations. Even in the semidarkness, the soft blue and white of an old bowl on the table, the faded red print of the hand-blocked curtains, still hanging at the windows, the jackets of the books on their shelves beside the fireplace, and the glow of brass candleholders and old copperware on the mantel and window ledge made him feel at home.

The prospect of having nothing to do for the next hours but read was intoxicating. He chose a small collection of books—some in Danish, some in English—and settled down. After an hour he stopped. He found he had been reading the same page over and over, with no idea of what was on it. It was impossible to stop thinking about what would happen next. He gave up and put the books back.

Then he discovered a shelf that must have belonged to a naturalist. There were books about stones and shells and all kinds of local plant and wild life. The color plates of birds and flowers and trees and the meticulously detailed descriptions of each species absorbed him completely.

Every half hour he would take a careful look out through the cracks in the shuttered windows. The landscape remained deserted except for an occasional child passing on his bicycle or a dog on the scent of a rabbit. A farmer rode into the village with milk and returned with empty cans clattering.

By one o'clock he had gone through birds, flowers, trees, and mushrooms, replaced all the books exactly where he had found them, and tied up the mattress on which he had rested so comfortably. The last bite of Mrs. Troner's chicken of the night before was gone. He made sure that no telltale evidence of his visit remained. Then, after scouting the surrounding territory as well as he could through the cracks in the shutters, he left the way he had come.

There was no sign of the rain that had threatened the night before. It was a brilliant Indian summer day. A fresh land breeze and the approaching end of the season would bring out every sailor for miles.

Karl got from the house to the beach as fast as he could and pulled his bicycle out of the deep grass edging the dune, where he had left it. He wheeled it clumsily through the loose sand until he reached the north edge of the village. There he could bring it up to the path that bordered the fields and ride it in the open. From the beach to the fork where he was to meet Timmy was only a few minutes' ride. He was ahead of schedule. With fifteen minutes to spare, he settled out of sight under the edge of the dune. The last juicy tomato relieved his thirst, which had bothered him ever since he left the cottage.

Little boats were coming out of their harbors, dipping, dodging, and pirouetting, in preparation for the afternoon's races. He could not linger safely much longer.

It was time to start. He lifted his bicycle up the ten or fifteen feet from the beach to the top of the dune and pushed off without looking back. He turned off the farm path from the shore onto the main road from the village. After the quiet byways, the usual traffic of Fynshav seemed to him as thick as rush hour in Copenhagen. Each time he heard an engine behind him, he was sure it was someone pursuing him. But one car after another passed without stopping or even slowing down. Before he knew it, the fork was almost ahead, and Timmy on his blue bike was wheeling toward him. When they met, Timmy said "Hi" and rode on without stopping. Karl followed. They said nothing. At the little dock they had built together on some land the Troners owned, Timmy opened his saddlebags and began transferring packages, carefully wrapped in oilskin, to the dinghy. Karl asked no questions. He rigged the boat. Timmy hoisted sail and then took the sheet. Karl cast off and settled down at the tiller. He pushed it over hard. Timmy tightened the sheet. The wind filled the sails. They were away. Now they could talk.

�֍ 5 �֍

The Race

"You have to leave this afternoon," Timmy began. "We didn't find out until after lunch yesterday. There wasn't time to wait until you and Peter found each other. We had to figure out messages for each of you that would bring you together so we could tell you what to do. The safest, surest way Father could think of was to go on with our racing plans."

It didn't sound very safe to Karl—to be racing in the middle of the open sound with half the families around Fynshav. But when he heard more about what had happened, he changed his mind.

Less than an hour after Karl had left the Troners' Thursday evening, Peter had knocked on the window of the headmaster's study. At first, the Troners sent him to the message center they'd told Karl to use. Then Mrs. Troner had second thoughts. "How will we know whether the boys find each other?" she said. "We can't leave messages in the same place. If Karl finds a note and takes it, Peter won't ever see it. If he reads it and puts it back, we won't be able to tell whether either of the boys has seen it."

To solve the problem, Mr. Troner directed Peter to go to a different spot on the north side of the village for his instructions.

Peter then left and went to the museum, hoping Karl would show up during the night. While he waited, Karl was out looking for him, and when Karl got back to the beech woods, it was too late for him to make the additional hitch up to the museum. By dawn both boys, following orders, had dropped out of sight without meeting.

There was an unexpected development that continued to keep them apart the following night. After breakfast Mrs. Troner climbed the hill as usual to open the museum. The day was such a lovely one that she took her knitting, planning to stay for a while after straightening up and dusting, just to enjoy the weather and the view.

She found no evidence that either of the boys had been there during the night. She was wondering what had kept them from taking shelter when she remembered the unused attic space where a double-decker bed had been set up one summer long ago for some temporary farm hands. The space—barely large enough for a fair-sized boy to turn around or stand up in—had not been used, even for storage, since, and no one had ever mentioned it to the boys. There was a winding, ladder-like stairway leading up from a narrow door behind the chimney. She decided to see whether the attic had been discovered. The door was unlocked. She climbed the hazardous steps cautiously to the tiny space under the roof. In the dim light everything seemed thick with cobwebs and dust, as if the place had been unvisited for years. But underneath the bottom bunk in full view was a plate. The remains of food on it were still moist. One of the boys had come and gone.

She decided to be on the safe side and put the dish where it wouldn't cause any questions. She tucked it into her bag, under the knitting, walked back down the hill to her own apartment in the school building, washed and dried it, then put it away with the china she kept on hand to use when she entertained in her own living room.

When she went back up the hill fifteen minutes later, two motorcycles were resting on their stands at the entrance. She heard footsteps inside. A moment later two Nazi officers, looking embarrassed as they usually did when they were discovered invading one's private property, came out from the stairway behind the fireplace.

They went off, muttering in broken Danish about missing persons. The incident left no doubt in the Troners' minds about the seriousness of Edlund's warning from Copenhagen.

Mrs. Troner knew that the men had not come from the local headquarters. They had tooled off in the direction of Sønderborg—the nearest town to the southwest. Still, this was no guarantee at all that they were gone for good. And for all she knew, they had alerted the Germans on duty in Fynshav before their visit to the museum.

The Troners had to warn the boys to keep away from the little museum. They decided to let Timmy be the messenger. A thirteen-year-old wandering aimlessly about the countryside would attract less attention than a grownup. But before Timmy had come back from delivering the first messages, another emergency developed.

Right after lunch the phone rang. It was Mrs. Troner's cousin in Kolding, not far from the end of the main route from Copenhagen to Jutland. Hardly waiting to hear how everyone in Fynshav was, she said: "The party for grandmother is tomorrow at five. Will you come?"

Mrs. Troner thanked her and promised they'd all be there. "They all" meant Peter and Karl. The invitation was not really an invitation. It was a code, and it gave Mr. Troner the prearranged signal to get the two boys to the five o'clock ferry from Mommark to Faaborg—the first stage of their second escape from the Nazis.

When Niels Holman had brought the letter from Edlund, he had also given Mr. Troner the preliminary instructions about Karl's route. Later the headmaster had planned how he would get both boys to the ferry when the word came for them to leave. But he had counted on their being together. Now, with little time to lose, he had to find a way to reunite them that he was sure they would understand and that he was equally certain would work. Escape by sailboat was the solution.

Timmy was the least suspicious guide they could have used.

Karl was told to join Timmy for the race as usual. Peter's note read: "Picnic and footrace at four." It would mean nothing to anyone who might conceivably find it, but it would be very clear to Peter. During the summer when Peter had been recovering from his illness, the boys had gone on picnics together at suppertime. When Karl got home from work, Timmy and Peter would have supplies ready, and they would all hike the short distance to a cove south of school. Here the beach was specially wide and sandy. Peter looked after the fire and the cooking, and Karl coached Timmy in his favorite sport—running—until supper was ready.

Karl and Tim were maneuvering the dinghy back and forth with the other sailors around the starting line now. The first gun for the race had been fired.

The start was now less than three minutes off. Timmy pulled out a stop watch. He seemed to have forgotten all about the danger they were in. They were silent, except for Tim's regular announcements—"Two minutes . . . one minute . . . 45 seconds . . . 30 seconds"—and Karl's occasional instructions: "Ready about. . . . We don't want to let her luff. . . . One more turn should do it."

The starting gun fired. The fleet was off before the wind on the first leg, south-southeast to a buoy in the sound. Karl and Timmy were well ahead at the start as usual—trying for a berth inside the buoy where they would be in a good position to round the marker for the second leg as narrowly as possible. Their lead widened as they paid out the sheet and the sail filled to bursting. Tim held out the boom with a whisker pole. There was too much wind to risk setting it in place. He preferred to watch it.

Not until they had rounded the mark and were on a beam course to the southwest did Timmy relax and get back to the business that occupied Karl's thoughts.

"Do you think Peter will get the idea and meet us at the cove?" Tim wanted to know.

Karl reassured him, but he knew *he* would feel much better when he saw Peter with his own eyes.

Timmy went on explaining the plan.

"Father said we should get mixed up in a bunch of boats right after the start of the last leg when we're near that marker close to shore. Then we should capsize or swamp."

"Timmy, you should have told me before. We're too far ahead now. It'll look funny if we slow up and get mixed in with the other boats." Karl was worried.

"But, Karl," Timmy pleaded, "it would have looked pretty phony if we had gotten off to a bad start with you at the tiller."

Karl couldn't help but smile at this spontaneous tribute.

"We can't do anything about it now, anyway. Let's just figure an excuse for slowing up."

Karl's superior knowledge of tides and currents solved the problem. Most sailors would think it best to continue on the inside as Karl and Tim had done on the first leg. But on this particular day's course, that was exactly the wrong thing to do. The second marker was almost directly off the mouth of a small stream that flowed between a large farm and the beech woods where Karl had slept on the night he had looked for Peter. The stream spilled into the bay and made a current, which, together with the ebbing tide, would exert considerable pressure against a boat trying to make a windward tack toward shore on the last leg to the finish line.

A smart sailor would make a turn well below the marker—avoiding the current, then tack to the east to get the benefit of current and tide as he sailed *away* from shore. Karl knew this.

"We'll stay right where we are," he said. "That way, the current at the marker will slow us up, and we'll be overtaken. No one will suspect us, then. They'll just think, 'This is one time we outsmarted them.' "

The plan worked. Just as they were rounding the mark, the current pushed them back downwind and over the course they had just covered. By the time they had managed to extricate themselves, half a dozen of the twenty boats in the race had caught up with them.

The rest was easy. Karl explained it. "We'll be pinching the boat a little too hard to make up for lost time. We'll jibe her wherever you say. They'll say, 'Just like those fools risking a jibe in this wind.' We'll go over, and the other boats will gloat. O.K.?"

Timmy nodded enthusiastically.

"But what's it all about? Then what?" Karl wanted to know.

Timmy continued recounting his father's instructions. "When the committee boat comes to help us, we're supposed to tell them we'll bail out on the beach.

The fleet sails on. We pull the boat ashore. We beach her at that spot where we had the picnic last summer. If Peter got our note, he'll be waiting for us."

If they were going to hit the spot Timmy had mentioned, they had to act quickly. They couldn't make another tack. Within yards of the six or seven lead boats, Karl gave the command: "Ready jibe."

A sudden puff hit them. The end of the boom struck the water, and in a second the sail was under, pulling the boat down. They were swamping.

Timmy called softly: "Be sure to make everything fast." Then he started swimming around after the floating gear. When the committee launch reached them, they were both on their feet walking the boat in. It was easy to wave off their rescuers. Eager to get out of the way of the second group of sailing dinghies that were fast approaching the mark, the motorboat withdrew.

Timmy said: "There're dry clothes Mom fixed for you and me in that bundle." He pointed to one of the rolls of oilskin that Karl had seen him take out of his saddlebag when they set out.

They searched the shoreline as they walked in to the beach. No sign of Peter—not a thing moving. They dragged the boat part way out of the water, then tipped it to drain enough water so that it would be light enough to turn over and empty. Shivering now from the chill wind on their wet clothes, they beached the boat, then stood, silent, to listen for any sound that might betray Peter's presence. The oaks and beeches bent before the west wind, but the grass and underbrush on the edge of the dunes were motionless. Karl opened the oil-skin and put on dry clothes. Timmy changed, too. They stowed their wet things. Still no sign of life. Finally Timmy said: "We can't wait much longer. You have to be on the five o'clock ferry."

"He may be waiting for the rest of the race to pass," Karl said.

"Or he may be waiting for us to join him in the woods."

"No one in the race would notice if I went up on the beach to look for Peter. They're all watching the finish," Karl said. He headed for the protected curve of land and water where the three boys had made their picnic fires in the summer and called.

No answer.

He waited under the shoulder of the dune. There was a stir in the bushes. He looked over. Around the silver trunk of a large beech, he saw black hair. A face peered cautiously out. All at once a body leaped down next to him. It was his friend—Peter.

"Keep close," Karl said. Covered by Karl's larger frame, Peter followed him down the fifty yards of beach to Timmy.

"Lie low," Karl commanded as Peter stepped into the dinghy. Timmy took the helm, and they pushed off.

"This is the bad part," Timmy said after they had been under way for a few minutes.

Instead of resuming the tacking pattern he would have had to follow to finish the race, he was turning the boat downwind. "We're not going to finish. We're going to hope everyone thinks we gave up and then forgets us in the excitement of the finish. We're going to sail out as if we were going back to harbor on a nice, easy long tack. But when everyone else is on the way home for supper, we're going to turn back toward shore and hot-foot it into that little harbor around the point." He pointed to the south. "Then I'll leave you and sail back."

"Can you make it back all right alone? It's a rough day to do it—with the wind almost dead ahead," Karl said.

If Timmy was worried, he didn't show it. "I'll stick close to shore. If it's taking too long, I'll pull in and tow her. Don't worry, some friend of Father's is going to watch."

After being alone for forty-eight hours, Peter was full of questions. Karl reported his movements of the past days, and Timmy told him about the narrow escape at the little museum.

"The longest hour I ever spent was the last one," Peter said. "I couldn't imagine where you'd be coming from or why. I even began to think the note was counter-feit—part of a plot to corner me. It never dawned on me that you'd be in that race, today of all times."

Timmy pointed to a cookie tin full of food and told them to eat for two days . . . just in case. Then he continued the instructions.

They would land a mile and a half from the ferry slip at Mommark. From there they were to walk along the beach. Five hundred yards before they hit the settle-ment, they would leave the beach and walk up to the main road, wait under cover until a few minutes before the ferry was to leave, then walk down to the village and go aboard.

The village was nothing more than a few scattered cottages, a small government building, and a one-room shed where the limited business of the ferry trade was transacted. The ferries came and went every three hours, carrying six or seven cars and about the same number of passengers, to Faaborg on the island of Fyn.

One or two Nazi guards were always on duty at the ferry slip. It would take bravado as well as courage to walk past them, but there was no other way.

Timmy pulled out their tickets.

Peter said: "Whew!"

After a few seconds Karl asked: "Then what?"

"You explore the boat the way anyone would when he first got aboard. You'll find a kind of lunchroom below deck, aft, and a small sort of bar, where you can sit and have a beer or something, on the top deck, fore. That's about it. At some point, while you're looking around, a sailor will attract your attention. You follow him."

As they sailed on, Timmy gave them the rest of their directions. They memorized the signals they were to look for and the responses they would have to make during each stretch of the trip to Copenhagen. By the time they were finished, the first part of the voyage seemed less formidable.

It was about four-thirty when they beached the boat again. There was no time to spare if they were to make the ferry. Timmy pulled the dinghy up so they could jump out without wetting their feet. He was still holding the line when Karl hugged him. "You make a pretty good captain for a fellow who says he can't. Be sure you keep up our record. See you, Tim."

Peter stuffed the remains of their meal in his pocket and shook hands. They didn't look back.

When they reached the main road overlooking the village, they could see smoke rising from the ferry's stack and hear the engines turning. The boat was loading. Without hesitating they walked down the hill and headed for the ticket collector on the edge of the slip. A blond woman surrounded by four yellow-haired children was struggling aboard, her arms loaded with bags of fall produce. Her parents were waving good-by from a farm wagon beside the dock.

The smallest child stumbled at the perfect moment. Karl picked him up. Peter took the hand of the little girl who had been trying to help her brother to his feet. Looking like a typical family group, they walked aboard, past the Nazi soldiers, who were much more interested in checking a wagon loaded with manure for the other shore.

The boys didn't wait to see whether the wagon got through.

They helped the young mother with her children up the steps to the restaurant-bar on the top deck and then began to look over the vessel as they had been told to do. They could feel the motion of the boat under them as they went down below again. They were away.

✸ 6 ✸

Finding the Leader

Karl and Peter went back down the short flight of steps from the café on the top deck. At the bottom a narrow passageway led off on either side to a slightly wider but equally dingy cabin, lighted only by the anemic glow from a shaded fixture over the bunk. The only furnishings were bare wooden benches, lined up like pews in a country chapel. They were understandably empty. Anyone but a recluse would have sought the warmth and comfort of the ferry's café, where food and drink and human voices might brighten the blackout and take the chill off the sea air.

The boys took the main staircase down to the loading deck. Still they passed no one. There was very little more to explore, and judging from the number of cars aboard, the ferry was traveling light.

There was a truck with the post office seal taped on its side: probably a farm vehicle that had been pressed

into service for the duration. The wagon loaded with
manure had apparently passed inspection. It was there,
creaking audibly as its sad old horse patiently shifted
his weight from one side to the other in an effort to find
comfort in the wagon shafts. There were a couple of
other passenger cars with no distinguishing marks to suggest the identity of their owners, and a motorcycle—obviously not official. That was all. The few passengers were
not in evidence. Probably they, too, were investigating
the ferry's café. Now and then Karl and Peter heard the
plop of rope hitting the deck, the heavier clank of a chain
dropping, or the splash of a wave against the hull. Except
for the steady rumble of the boat's engines, there were no
other sounds.

The boys walked aft and stood watching as the boat
turned north for the crossing. The propellers churned
the gentle waters of the bay into a great lather in the
ferry's wake. Already the little dock they had left was
barely distinguishable from the other landings scattered along the shore. They could trace the road they
had just come over to the point where it rounded the
bend and disappeared behind the fields.

"I wonder if Timmy's home now," Karl said. It was
the first time either of them had spoken since they had
stepped out of cover onto the road above Mommark.

Peter turned toward the spot on the shore where they
had parted. "The wind's changed," he said.

Karl was looking, too. With the motion of the boat,
it was hard to feel any breeze at all. But when he looked
carefully, he could see that what wind there was came
off the water. As often happens at sunset after a warm

day, the cooler air over the water was moving in toward the warmer air over the land, and the breeze had shifted.

"That will make it easier for Tim. He's probably home by now," Karl said, continuing to scan the western horizon.

"I see him—look, Karl—just below the cove. See?" Peter said.

"Of course it's Tim. It has to be with that red telltale against his mast. He hasn't used it since the first week he sailed. He can judge the wind direction quicker than I can. He's put it on so we could spot him." Karl was pleased.

On the fast receding shoreline, they could just make out the little dinghy with the spot of red topping the mast. "He's not moving. I bet he anchored to wait for us. What a kid!" Peter said.

They watched until even the red speck had disappeared from sight and then walked through the boat, past the cars and the horse—now almost asleep—to the fore deck. Perhaps the growing coolness of the evening air had made the passengers take cover. No one—not even the sailor they were expecting—was in sight. The captain and mate were in the pilothouse above them. The anchor lines and chains were neatly coiled. They were heading steadily and surely across the sound, toward the gentle dunes of the island, golden now in the glow of the dropping sun.

The only part of the ferry left to be investigated was the lunchroom below the deck. They found the stairway midships and started down the ladder-like steps, Karl leading. The room was opposite the bottom of the stairs. Karl had his hand on the door when a sailor appeared as if from nowhere.

"Let me show you my cabin?" He spoke quietly, but there was no mistaking the command in his voice. Without waiting for an answer, he turned away from the lunchroom. They followed.

Once inside his cabin, the sailor shut the door and motioned Karl and Peter to a bunk. They had no choice but to sit down. In the space between the bunks, there was really no room to stand. The sailor took the only chair and without introduction began to talk.

"You're probably perfectly safe on board, but you might as well stay here. Rest while you can. I'll try to bring some coffee before we land."

The boys were sitting close enough to touch each other. From the time they had met on the beach, they had been moving together, almost in unison, gaining courage from each other. Now Peter got up and went over to the other bunk.

"Have you any instructions?" he asked the sailor.

"I don't know where you came from or where you're going or who you are. But I have this."

He pulled a brown parcel, no bigger than a letter, out of his pocket and handed it to Peter.

"I must get back on duty," he said, and left quickly.

They opened the envelope eagerly. Inside was a smaller envelope, plainly marked with instructions for use.

Both boys burst into almost hysterical laughter. It was red hair dye. A knock on the door shocked them back to silence. They looked at each other in horror, not knowing what to do or where to go. There was not a sound outside the door. They held their breaths. Five minutes must have passed. The door of the lunchroom down the passageway opened. There were men's voices, then footsteps on the metal stairs, and again silence.

Another short interval and the cabin door opened. The sailor came in, bringing steaming mugs. "Did I scare you when I went past? I meant to. It's not normal for sailors to be laughing in their bunks when we're under way. You don't want to attract attention."

"Thanks," Karl said. "We were crazy to forget."

Peter pulled out the dye. "It was this," he said, showing it to the sailor, who smiled when he saw the glamorous redhead pictured on the envelope and tried to imagine the boys before him with their heads dyed "siren red."

"I guess the idea was to make us look like Danes," Karl said.

"Show me a Dane with hair like that?" Peter asked rhetorically.

"It may be the best an amateur can do to make black hair look Danish-blond. They must think siren red looks less non-Aryan than brunette," Karl suggested.

"It's crazy," was Peter's vehement reply. "If that phony color didn't give me away, my embarassment would. Let's ditch it." He looked for approval to his companions.

"I agree." Karl's response was enthusiastic. The sailor nodded consent.

With that, Peter carefully washed the dyestuff down the drain of the cabin's tiny washbasin and handed the empty envelope to the sailor.

"You can probably get rid of this more easily than we could. I'd hate to be caught with it."

The sailor stuffed the packet into his pocket and started for the door. "I'll knock twice when it's time to land. If I get a chance, I'll bring coffee again."

He was gone before they had thanked him. It was strange what reassurance his presence gave them. Once more alone, they were at first afraid to speak. Then in whispers they began reviewing the details of their route.

There would be hours more before they could count on any kind of safety after they left the ferry. They would have to find out when the train left for Nyborg across the island of Fyn. It was a minor line. Wartime train schedules were chaotic at best. If they had a long wait, they'd have to decide whether to look for a bus route or take a chance on hitchhiking. Tim's instructions did not cover these details. The uncertainty made them uncomfortable. Problems that had not occurred to them before seemed insurmountable. If they had to wait for the train, where could they go? Would it be simpler to settle down in a café until traintime or find a hiding place?

"We should have thought of some of these little questions before we let our friend go," Peter said.

"He'll be back." Karl was surprised that his voice sounded so calm. "Let's think about something else."

Peter pulled out a miniature checker set. For once it

was a welcome sight to Karl. "Where did you get that?" he asked.

"It was a farewell present from Mr. Larsen. He must have guessed we'd need it."

They settled down to the usual unequal contest in which Peter was always the winner. Karl was involved in the play, too, which was not always so. When the sailor's double knock sounded, both boys bolted to their feet. This time he brought cake with the coffee.

"You fellows have nerves of steel," he said. "Didn't you notice we'd landed? Weren't you afraid I'd forgotten you?"

As the sailor spoke, the engines died and the boat seemed completely still.

"I think you can walk off safely now. Even the captain's gone home. In a minute the harbor lights will be off and only the rigging lights will be burning."

"What about the train?" Karl asked.

"You know as much as I do," the sailor replied. True to his word, he was not giving information or advice.

"Shall we wait in a hotel or is there a café?" Peter asked.

"I can only repeat, 'Don't attract attention.' "

"Are there many guards?" Karl persisted, hardly hoping for a useful reply.

From the sailor's expression, they could see that he would like to help. "How can I say? It's all new. We've had little trouble before. You know what you're to do. Be yourselves."

He said good-by and ushered them out. He followed

them up the stairs and led them to the gangway. They heard him fasten the chain across it as they walked off onto the dock. Through the pitch black, they could see the vague outline of a building a few hundred yards to the left. Hoping it was the railroad station that Tim had described to them, they headed toward it. They had gone but a short way when they heard someone running behind them. It was the sailor.

"Keep over to the side for a few minutes. I may be able to help you," he said.

They were passing a shed that might have housed the ferry's ticket office. They flattened themselves against the harbor side of the building, away from the path and waited. Five minutes, ten minutes must have passed. They heard a train's engine gathering steam. Could it be their train? Would they make it? When would there be another? Why wouldn't the sailor answer their questions? Was he really helping or was he a *stikker,* a Dane in league with the Nazis, out to trap them? They were torn between making a bold dash for the train and trusting the man they had been told to follow.

They heard voices, then footsteps in the sandy path. The accent was unmistakably German. Silence. Then another voice. It was the sailor. No question about it. And, no question, either, about his mission. He talked louder than he needed to. Every syllable was audible to Karl and Peter.

"It won't take a minute for me to find them," he was saying. "The passenger didn't give me her name. She just explained you were a friend and asked me to give you this package. She'd been staying with her parents in Sønderborg. They're farmers. I'd let it go until morning, but I know there was butter and eggs in it and they might not keep."

The other man interrupted. "You're very kind. But I'm supposed to go through the train again before it leaves."

The sailor replied: "But it will pull out any minute and you *have* been through, just now, have you not?"

"You're right. There probably won't be anyone else boarding this late. I won't worry." The German dismissed the subject.

They saw his uniform as he passed. A minute later the chain clanked again as the sailor opened the way for the Nazi guard to board the ferry to get his package. Without exchanging a word, Karl and Peter made a dash for the train, puffing away beyond the station, not two minutes distant.

The guard never knew that two young men got on the train while he was picking up his provisions on the ferry that night. The sailor could only hope they made it.

✺ 7 ✺
The Contact

It was a typical farmer's train—the kind that travels at a snail's pace through rural areas, stopping on signal to pick up farmers or their produce bound for market. It carried more produce than passengers as it traveled eastward toward the population center of Denmark. The one passenger car was empty.

Karl and Peter settled themselves in a compartment far down the corridor from the entrance. Not a moment after they had made themselves comfortable, the conductor called the starting signal to the engineer. There was a series of preliminary groans and jerks. Then the wheels began to turn. They were off on the second leg of their journey.

As is often the case on slow night trains, the conductor's primary objective was to get a good night's rest. He sold them their tickets to Nyborg. But almost before they had put away their change, he had retired to the end compartment, clanged the door shut behind him, and sunk into a sonorous sleep.

That was the most sensible course for anyone to follow in the enforced blackout. But the excitement of the past hours and the tension of the moment made sleep unthinkable for Karl and Peter. They sat silently with their thoughts and anxieties. The train rolled on smoothly enough. For all the signs of human life they saw, they might have been its only occupants.

Gradually they began to feel at home. After a while Peter made a scouting trip down the corridor and reported all well. Karl followed him. Another fifteen minutes passed and the train slowed. The conductor pulled open the door and stumbled down the steps to the platform. A routine exchange of greetings took place. A single passenger boarded and took a place near the entrance. The train pulled on again and stopped twenty minutes later to load chickens and boxes of eggs and vegetables. By the end of the first hour of stops and starts and pauses, the boys found they could doze between stations. In fact, Karl must have relaxed more completely than he thought possible. He started at the sound of the compartment door being pulled open. They had a companion.

Sleep now seemed the best escape. Karl burrowed deeper into his corner of the compartment and tried to continue his nap. It was soon clear that even if his nerves would let him, his new companion would not. He was a fussy man. It took him five minutes to decide whether the compartment door should be open wide, shut tight, or left with just a slit for ventilation. Karl and Peter's pretense of being asleep grew less credible as the new-comer continued bustling about.

He was bound to rouse them. He lighted a large cigar and shut the compartment door tight. Two stops later he put out the cigar and began crackling papers. The telltale fragrances of sausages and cheese announced a midnight supper. It was pointless to pretend further. In fact, it was impossible.

"Come on, boys," the traveler called in a booming voice. "Wake up. My wife has packed enough for a banquet." He pushed a crusty slice of peasant bread thick with butter and topped with a good slab of paté toward Peter and enthusiastically began preparing another for Karl.

There was no need to worry about the risk of getting into conversation with him. As long as they accepted what he offered, their host was perfectly happy to do all the talking himself.

He rambled on about the price of eggs. (He was going to the city to negotiate the sale of his hay crop.) He recounted in lavish detail his slow but steady accumulation of land, accomplished through hard work, shrewd bargaining, and his wife's skill in making one krone do the work of two.

He forced his life on them just as he did a steady stream of cheese (from his own herd), bread (from his wife's oven), cake (from her recipe and their eggs and butter). Finally, even he was approaching his capacity.

He made a last effort to persuade them to have one more sliver of cake, then sadly, and with loving care, he rewrapped his provisions and packed them back into the basket his wife had given him.

The feast had gone on through numerous stops and starts as the night train from Faaborg slowly wended its way to its terminal in Nyborg. A few passengers had gotten on along the route, but the extensive trappings of the feast and the luggage that occupied and overflowed the racks above their seats had discouraged anyone from joining them.

Peter was nodding and jerking himself to attention, trying to resist the urge to relax completely into sleep. Karl began to nod, too. If he didn't know when they'd get to Nyborg or where they'd go when they did, there was no use fretting about it now.

The big farmer lighted another cigar. It smelled rich and comfortable. The restful motion of the car and the regular rackety-rack of the wheels on the rails was lulling Karl to sleep. Anticipation of the next day's business, however, seemed to have a stimulating effect on the farmer. He began to talk again. It was as hard to ignore him as it was to fend off his food. He had exhausted his store of information about himself and finally become curious about them.

His sons were at home minding the farm. Why were *they* out traveling at this hour of the night, he wanted to know.

It was Peter who took up the challenge. His assurance surprised him. He took his time answering. His mind worked slowly, as if he were planning a school composition. If one idea for an answer didn't suit him, he discarded it and tried another before putting it into words.

Karl kept quiet. He was too drowsy to be inventive. And he knew Peter would compose a better story alone. This was Peter's forte. At school he could invent situations and dialogue endlessly, keeping the audience roaring with laughter from start to finish. The present crisis required no such ingenuity. Anything Peter said about himself or Karl only stimulated the farmer to a new spate of bragging about his own affairs.

Peter explained that their grandfather had been very ill and that their parents had been with him in Copenhagen for the past week. They had phoned only yesterday to ask the boys to come.

The farmer droned on about his sons. He didn't even think to be sympathetic with the boys' impending bereavement. His boys had never been to Copenhagen. In fact, they had never been five miles from home, except once—when they went to the Folk High School in Fynshav. "Ever been there?" he asked Peter, who might just as well have been struck by lightning.

Karl's mind jumped to attention. "We're not far from there," Peter said calmly, sure that his voice trembled. "But we're town people. My father's a builder in Padborg on the border."

"I know it well," the farmer came back. "My cousin has a farm close by. It must be miserable so near the border. You don't know who's your friend and who's a Nazi, I bet."

Karl didn't dare look at the man's face. He noticed

with relief that the train was slowing up for the stop. He nudged Peter. "Come on. We're pulling in," he said.

They began to move the farmer's luggage to the entrance platform with courtly deference. It gave them an excuse to ignore his last remarks about the Nazis.

"Too bad we can't talk some more," the farmer said. "We must have many friends in common. I'm Christian Bergman. My cousin's Møller. Know him?"

Peter guessed wildly. "I think my father's done some work for him. He's on the north side of town, isn't he?"

The train stopped. The door opened. They started down the platform to the station, all three of them carrying Mr. Bergman's luggage. "You haven't told me *your* name. I'll have to tell my cousin when I see him."

"It's Møller, too," Peter answered, laughing. It was a perfect name—the most common he could think of. Not that it would matter. By the time the farmer got a chance to tell his cousin, they would be far from Padborg.

Outside the station the streets were empty. In a minute a taxi, guided only by its parking lights, inched up to the curb. Mr. Bergman climbed in, and they piled his bags and bundles around him. They declined his offer of a lift, explaining that their hotel was nearby.

"I don't like to have you go off by yourselves. You may be stopped. Sometimes you won't see a guard for miles. But if there's any truth in these rumors about arresting the Jews, there may be more around tonight. You shouldn't have any trouble, though, even if they do stop you. Show them your papers. If they aren't satisfied, you know where I am. Call me. We'll see how some of my Anne's sausage will soften them up. They haven't had any decent food for years. All right?"

He was still laughing at his own joke when the taxi pulled off. Peter stood frozen until it rounded the corner. Then both boys gave themselves up to hysterical laughter. Karl praised his friend's performance, but they were both glad it was over. It was safer traveling alone, they decided, even without Anne's sausage.

They had been in Nyborg but once before—passing through on their first trip from Copenhagen to Jutland. They remembered that the ferry wharves were close to the station, just as they were in Faaborg. The instructions they'd been given began to run through Karl's mind. "Take the morning boat for Korsør. There is a hotel in Nyborg where you might be expected. It is a hundred yards south of the ferry slip—down a narrow street, Kierkegade—the third house on the right. On a sign painted white, you'll see the name, Sailor's Harbor. Go in. Ring the bell. The clerk will be wearing a blue shirt with an orange marigold in the button hole. You say: 'We missed the boat. We need a room off the street.' He'll give you bed and breakfast. Wait for him to tell you when to leave."

They picked their way down the cobblestoned street, walking steadily but slowly, watching for guards who might question their being out after dark. There was nothing stirring. A thick fog was moving in from the water. The night was clammy and uncomfortable.

Peter had not complained, but Karl could see that he was favoring his bad leg. He suppressed the fear that

Peter's illness might recur. They would be safe and away, he told himself to fire his courage. They must hurry.

Deserted for the night, the ferry loomed large and dark over the little fishing boats that bobbed at their moorings. If there was a guard, he was quiet as the dock itself—asleep against a piling, perhaps, or warming himself at some harborside bar.

They found the man with the marigold without any trouble. He showed them to a tiny room with a big bed. They were almost asleep in its downy vastness when he knocked at the door and came in with glasses of a hot and pungent liquor, heavily laced with lemon, spice, and sugar. After their short walk in the damp night, it was welcome. They drank it and fell asleep. When he knocked again, it was broad daylight. They were still hurrying through the rolls and coffee he had brought them when he returned to tell them to go at once.

"You know the way," he said. That was all.

✲ 8 ✲

The Man in the Cotton Coat

They had gone no farther than the entrance to the broad
street fronting the harbor when they realized that the
risks they had faced at first no longer existed. At home
they were afraid of being picked up because they were
so well known. When they were off home grounds, they
were still in danger. In the sparsely settled country
through which they had come, any traveler stood out
simply because travel itself was so rare. Now the danger
had changed.

The streets were thick with a confusion of men and
women and boys and girls hurrying to market or to work
or to school, on foot, on bicycles, or with carts. Bicycle
bells jangled as their impatient owners tried to make
headway. Pushcart operators shouted for pedestrians to
make way. Oblivious of the turmoil around them, an occasional couple walked along at their own unhurried
pace, absorbed in conversation.

They could certainly walk down the street totally unnoticed by the population of Nyborg, which seemed too engrossed in its own affairs at this hour of day to notice even a friend. But in all this bustle, Karl suspected, the lookout for Jews would be much sharper. To the trained eye of a Nazi agent, who could tell what subtle quality of complexion, build, feature, or movement might not appear suspicious. Karl, trying to be optimistic, decided he might possibly be fair enough to pass as a true Dane. But Peter—if his jet black hair was not enough to make him "foreign"—was bound to attract attention with his limp.

As if Peter had been reading his mind, he spoke: "Karl, if you see I'm favoring that damn leg, tell me. I think I can stop doing it."

Karl nodded agreement. "We'll be all right. It's just till we get aboard."

"I can hold out. The boat should be loading now."

They were coming to the dock. According to their instructions, they should find the ticket seller in a stall to the left of the gangway. Peter spotted it first and nudged Karl. There was a line. They decided to get lost in the crowd. It wouldn't do to expose themselves by waiting.

When the queue had dwindled to three, Peter retired to make an exhaustive survey of the pushcart wares on the edge of the ferry slip.

Karl was stuck behind an old lady. The first two people in the line got their tickets, put down their money, and were off without delay. But it seemed as if the old woman would never be on her way. Waiting nervously,

Karl's eyes caught sight of Peter. He was looking even more anxious than Karl felt. At the top of each passenger ramp was a soldier in uniform. Just when Karl saw them, the one on the left looked up. There were twenty-five yards and a milling crowd of tradesmen and passengers between them, but their eyes met. It was too late to turn away, Karl knew, and he felt his face redden and his breath catch.

Boldly he stared ahead at the SS guard, praying that his panic didn't show. It seemed minutes, but it could not have been more than a second or two. At last the man looked down at the passengers approaching him.

For the moment Karl forgot him. The woman ahead had purchased her ticket and was burrowing in the folds of a large shopping sack for money. She finally extracted it, but she had miscalculated. The whole process began again. Once the transaction was completed, she had questions. When would the ferry arrive? When did the train leave from Korsør for Copenhagen? Satisfied at last, she showered the ticket seller with thanks so profuse it took almost as much time as the purchase had.

Finally, gathering up her possessions, she went on. Karl had given his order and proffered his money. Tickets in hand, he joined Peter, just at the approach to the gangway. The passenger ramps were on either side of the auto track. He whispered: "We better take the right side."

The black-uniformed men at the top of each ramp seemed unruffled, eyes riveted on the faces approaching them. Not a single passenger greeted them or even looked their way.

Karl's heart jumped. As if from the blue, the guard on the left whose eye had caught his a moment before reached out and stopped a woman. Karl pushed Peter ahead. "Let's not go together," he whispered. Now he was sure he would never get aboard. He was convinced the other guard had marked him and would signal his companion to stop him.

He bent down as if to pick up something he had dropped. A split second later he started up the gang-plank. Peter had already passed the guard and disappeared aboard. Stepping up that ramp was like walking off a roof. He could not believe it when he found himself aboard. He didn't dare look back until he had climbed to the upper deck and caught sight of Peter ahead, looking over the rail.

There was a fifteen-minute wait before the boat weighed anchor. But already there seemed to be half again as many passengers aboard as it was designed to carry. The bars were full. The cafeteria lines in the dining room reached well out into the corridors. There was a holiday atmosphere in the crowd that Peter and Karl enjoyed after the quiet air of the country where they had been for the last two years. They almost forgot why they were there.

In one corner some boys and girls were singing to the accompaniment of a banjo. At another table close by the windows that lined the sides of the big dining saloon, half a dozen men were talking and laughing noisily as they enjoyed their coffee and morning cigars.

Peter and Karl moved around the ship looking for the signal they had been told to expect. But with a good two and a half hours of sea travel ahead, there was no urgency. The sun was making one of its rare early fall appearances. They took advantage of the rush for the dining rooms to find themselves deck chairs in the open, where they could watch the water and relish the sun in comfort.

People were settling down. The bell, signaling the imminent raising of the gangplank, had been clanging fiercely for several minutes. A few stragglers were running to avoid being left on the dock. Sailors at their posts were catching lines tossed by the men on the dock and coiling them at their feet. Children were racing each other to get the last of the deck chairs for their parents. A group of schoolgirls stopped and asked where the dining room was. Peter pointed the way but advised them they'd have a long wait and invited them to stick around on deck until the crowd thinned out.

Karl was startled at first by Peter's bold gesture. Then he realized he was witnessing just one more sample of his friend's cleverness. Nothing could have made them look more natural than to surround themselves with half a dozen girls—all laughing and talking at once. Each one of them answered any question either Karl or Peter put to them simultaneously. They were off on a school trip to Copenhagen and Elsinore with their teacher, who—of course—was holed up in some quiet corner with a book, preparing their tours.

Nothing could have given the girls more pleasure than

this chance to describe the anguish and hardship of boarding-school life and food. It never occurred to one of them to be curious about the boys. They were either too young or too shy or—more likely—too interested in their own existence.

The boat sailed. The sun made its customary retreat, and once again the chill and penetrating mist obscured the sea and the receding shore. One could tell from the file of passengers promenading around the deck that the dining room would be emptying. It was a good time to break the journey.

The girls piled their books and raincoats on the chairs to advertise their claim, and the boys led the way to the dining room. The choice of food had thinned along with the crowd, but the menu hardly mattered. A girl with dark curly hair and blue eyes gave an imitation of her history teacher's peculiar way of going to the blackboard or leaving the room without turning her eyes from the class. Every move she made reduced her friends to paroxysms of laughter.

Her performance was followed by another, and so on, until the girls had described their entire faculty in pantomine.

Suddenly a hush fell. There was no need for Karl and Peter to look up. The girls' chaperone had obviously been sighted. Karl and Peter sprang to their feet and bowed. The lady, whom her students had described as an old spinster, could not have been over thirty. She asked the boys to stay. But the fun was over. They excused themselves, saying they had reading to do.

Instead of returning to the deck, they found a quiet

corner in a smaller saloon on the lower deck. Peter bought some cards and began to deal a pinochle hand. In the midst of picking up his hand, Karl stopped. A man had walked past from behind, crossed the room without stopping, slowly, deliberately opened the sliding door on the other side, and left. When he raised his hands to push open the door, there was something on his finger—something white on his little finger. Was it their leader?

Karl glanced at the clock over the bar and finished picking up and sorting his hand. He said nothing. There was still a full hour. They played one hand after another. Karl was winning. He was ready to quit. Peter tried the gamesman's usual dodge. "Quit when you're winning, eh? That'll be the first time in eight months you've been ahead. One more game?"

Karl agreed.

Halfway through, just as if he were saying, "I'll take this one with my king," Karl said quietly: "I think I saw our man. Shall we go?"

Peter didn't answer—not until the last card was played. "There you go," he said, raking in the last trick. "That'll change things a bit, won't it?" He bent over the score, adding carefully, then announced the verdict. "Remember that's just for today," he said. Then he rose and walked toward the sliding door.

Just as they left the room, they saw their man in the corridor. He was unmistakable. His hat was pulled down—not too far. The cotton raincoat was belted but unbuttoned. He raised his left hand to stifle a cough. Tied around the little finger was a bandage made from a man's handkerchief. They passed each other in silence, without any sign of recognition.

Back at the abandoned deck chairs, they found the jackets they had left, but the girls and their belongings had disappeared. Only a few hardy country men and women—the old-fashioned type who walk the decks in all weather as a kind of health insurance—continued their lonely, dogged circling of the ferry, bundled against the damp in waterproofs, hooded coats, or shawls.

Karl and Peter joined the promenade, but by the end of the first round, the moisture seemed to have reached their bones. The boat's horn sounded intermittently in the fog—the loneliest sound in the world. Occasionally they heard the answering foghorn from some rock or buoy. Soon it began to sound at regular intervals. The moan grew closer. They were nearing port.

They made their way slowly back up to the upper deck. By then the noise of the foghorn was uncomfortably penetrating. Through the murk they could just distinguish the vague skyline of Korsør ahead. The guiding lights on the dock shone sickly through the thick mist. It would be hard to recognize a friend at more than a few paces. The man in the cotton coat was nowhere to be seen. It was a lonely feeling.

Now the movement was toward the bow. There was a bump and a jar, then the creaking adjustment of the vessel's planks and ribs as she came to rest; a brief shudder of the dying engine and they were safely in port.

The boys were almost lost in the push of passengers down the stairs to the landing deck and off the gangway. They could be sure that the main stream of traffic would be toward the station, where trains left in every direction for the cities and towns of Denmark's populous eastern island. They were carried along, almost bodily, by the force of the crowd. The only comfort was the realization that anyone looking for them would have as much trouble spotting them as they were having simply keeping track of each other.

The bright lights inside the station were a welcome relief from the blanket of fog they had just left. Their eyes turned to the board that listed arrivals and departures. There were three trains for Copenhagen—not one. An express to the city limits, a train that made limited stops, and the local—taking almost the entire day to cover the sixty-five-mile journey.

They were afraid to appear hesitant. They looked at each other. Each knew what the other was thinking without speaking. Karl started to walk. "Come on," he said, leading the way in the direction of the local.

Once out of the crush, he said: "I have a hunch this is right."

"Why?" Peter asked.

"Fewer through passengers. We'll attract less attention."

"That was my guess," Peter said.

The train was long—maybe fifteen cars. They chose one close to the engine, got on, and sat down. Few other passengers bothered to walk so far down the platform. The car seemed almost empty when the train pulled out. They were not eager to talk. There was no point in putting their thoughts into words. For the time being there was only one worry. Had they chosen correctly? Until they caught sight of their leader, they would not know.

✿ 9 ✿

The Pancake Party

It was a long ride, the sixty-five-mile journey across the island of Zealand, made longer by the constant stops to let off freight and passengers and take up new people and cargo. The circumstances of the trip did not help to make it pass more quickly.

The boys' thoughts were on the unknown ahead. Where was the man in the cotton coat? Where would he take them? If they didn't see him, if—to be perfectly plain and blunt—he wasn't even on this particular train, which they had picked rather arbitrarily after all, what next?

These were not questions to discuss on a public conveyance traveling at the measured speed of ten miles or so an hour across the meadowlands and industrial sprawl of wartime Denmark. So they dozed, played an occasional listless game of cards, and all the while kept

a sharp if surreptitious watch on what was happening
outside their compartment window.

The train was filling up. By the end of the first hour
of the trip, a few people got as far as their car looking
for seats. Before they had been traveling two hours, the
traffic back and forth was almost constant. A mother
hurried past with a small child in tow, obviously going
to the bathroom. Then minutes later another woman
passed, holding a crying child whose best suit was drip-
ping with milk.

A vendor passed through with sandwiches and candy.
They bought everything he offered, just to pass the
time. Men with cigars came out of their compartments
and congregated in the corridor, smoking and exchanging tidbits from the inexhaustible small talk they seem
to store for such occasions.

Sometimes a man or woman, or a schoolgirl or boy of
their own age, passed back or forth, watching the other
passengers, peering into the compartments as they went
by—just as Karl or Peter might have done if the trip had
been an ordinary one for them.

Karl knew from the conversation he had overheard at
the ticket window in Nyborg that the express took over
three hours. Their trip would be twice as long. The
sun, which had been playing hide and seek with the fog
all day, was falling behind them now and seemed about
to give up the effort to shine at all. It was going to be
another damp and black misty evening. Night would fall
probably even before they reached their destination—
whatever it might be.

The countryside now was more populous. Each time

the train slowed up for a stop, there were scores of people waiting on the platforms.

They were beginning to see uniforms. There were officers and soldiers both. Perhaps they were going off guard duty at the factories one could see from the train and returning to quarters in Copenhagen, or heading for a night on the town. There were special-forces men among them. Even out of uniform, their watchful posture was easy to spot if you were looking for it. The usual soldiers off duty were in pairs or groups, talking and laughing together or clinging to each other in uncomfortable isolation from the civilians whose land they were "in" but not "of." The special troops paced up and down or stood silent, motionless, detached—always alone. Sometimes one would board the train and disappear from Karl's view among the workmen and women going home from work or traveling on unknown missions of business or pleasure to the capital.

By the most generous estimate, they had at least half an hour more to travel. The train was just picking up speed after its last stop. The corridors were still alive with voices, footsteps, the opening and shutting of doors as the new passengers found seats. The compartment door swung open with a bang. A middle-aged man of medium height was in the entrance. His expression said "May I?" though he uttered not a word. The boys nodded quickly. He edged into the corner of the seat facing forward and stared straight ahead. Beneath the workman's cap pulled down across his face, his hair showed "siren red." It was even more bizarre than Karl had imagined. The man looked like a circus clown suddenly called to a funeral. Karl looked at Peter. Peter began to smile, and at once all their self-control vanished. Peter left the compartment abruptly to conceal his giggling and pull himself together. Fear for their safety brought Karl back to instant attention. The incident was over just in time. Peter had hardly settled down in his seat again when the door opened behind him. It was a pair of German soldiers who were looking for seats.

The boys sat like prisoners, immobilized, waiting for the executioner's blow. Karl could feel his red-headed seatmate cringe into his shadowy corner. Silently he thanked God that the blackout would leave the compartment too dimly lighted for the dyed hair to be noticeable.

The soldiers were old men, clearly not fit for combat. Karl pressed against the wall and kept his eyes on the windows across the corridor. Peter was squeezed into the corner next to the door by the Germans, whether he liked it or not. The two men sat down and smoked and talked, nipping now and then from a small flask that they passed back and forth.

The smell of cheap liquor and tobacco was almost distracting enough to chase any other thoughts from his mind. But Karl had one ear cocked—following the soldiers' conversation.

Lonely and homesick, they were talking of their families. The older, quieter man had lost one son in Russia. His younger boy had been wounded in Italy—wounded beyond recovery. The second soldier without giving names or ages or details said simply, "Mine are all gone."

At that moment Karl found it hard to remember they

were the enemy. The men had stopped talking. In need of some distraction, they looked up to see who was sharing their compartment. Karl braced himself for the inspection and looked stiffly out to the corridor, sure that his nervousness showed.

Preoccupied as he was, he almost overlooked a man walking by. It was a tiny detail that caught his eye—a white bandage on the little finger of the left hand. Now he had passed. Was he the slight man of medium height? He had on a cotton coat—but almost every Dane wore a cotton coat during the war. Was it buttoned or simply belted? It was too late to tell.

Karl stole a glance at Peter. It was impossible to discover whether his friend had noticed anything. Had the man's bandaged hand seemed to beckon? Karl decided fast. The train was pulling to a stop. He got up casually, opened the door slowly, shut it behind him, and walked down the corridor without a backward look. He heard a door open and shut, then steps behind him. Still he did not look back. Many passengers were preparing to get off. The train braked to a sharp stop.

Karl hopped down to the platform with a dozen or more other passengers from his car. He took a look up and down, searching for the exit.

Not far to the right, a young woman in a dark trench coat was greeting a man. For a second the fellow turned back toward the train, paused as if looking for his baggage, then took her arm and started toward a long flight of stairs farther up the platform. It was the man Karl had seen first on the ferry—the man in the cotton raincoat. There was no mistaking the signal.

Before he had made up his mind whether it was wise to wait, he was jostled by someone passing. Peter had caught up and overtaken him. Now it was Karl's turn to follow him down the platform. There must have been almost a hundred people milling around. The sign on the station house read "Valby." The name meant nothing. It was almost dark. Already the greenish glow of the dimmed street lamps through the misty twilight cast a weird light on people and things. The street was almost empty except for the passengers from the train, who took their separate ways from the top of the stairs. Karl could just make out the figures of their leaders walking unhurriedly down the sidewalk across the street some fifty feet ahead.

After the almost unpopulated meadowlands of Jutland, this seemed a thickly settled city. The street was lined with three- or four-story houses, built right to the sidewalk. Dotted among them were small shops, most of them already closed for the night.

They must have gone a block or two. They could see a square opening up a hundred yards beyond their guides. Without warning the man in the cotton coat made an abrupt about face, took off his slouch hat, turned toward his companion, made a deep bow, and hurried off down a side street to the right. Without a pause the girl continued in the direction they had been going. The finality of the man's gesture made it clear that his mission was complete. They followed the girl.

She led them across the open square and down a pretty street to the left. Some of the houses were brick,

some stone; some were straight, and some had slanted
roofs with white dormer windows and flower boxes. The
girl opened the door of one of them and shut it behind
her. There were half a dozen people walking at intervals
behind her, including Karl and Peter. The first one—a
man—followed her path. A few seconds later a woman
entered the same door. Peter was next. Karl saw the
gray door close behind him. Two more pedestrians
walked past. A third stopped and went into the house
after Peter. Karl felt that he was followed, but he dared
not look behind him. He was next. The handle was in
his hand. It was like starting on stage to address an
auditorium full of schoolmates and teachers. The mixture of anticipation and fright was pleasure and pain at
once. The hallway he entered was darker than the
street. Before he had gotten his bearings, the door he
had just shut behind him opened. Someone bumped
him, but no one spoke. He could hear the person's rapid
breathing. As Karl's eyes adjusted to the dark, he saw a
slit of light ahead. He moved toward it. The person behind him moved, too. There was a door. He opened it
and walked into the dining room of someone's apartment where a boy of nine or ten was doing his homework
at a big table. The child looked up and pointed across the
room. A door led to the kitchen, where a woman was busy
cooking. She smiled, dropped what she was doing, and
opened the back door of the house—gesturing across
what seemed to be an enclosed court to a shed.

Karl nodded his thanks and went on to the outbuild-
ing. There in the candlelight he found more than half a

dozen men and women including the girl who had been their guide. He heard his name called. Then Peter was beside him.

Behind a voice said: "I frightened you back there, didn't I? I'm sorry."

It was the man with the flaming hair who had been with them on the train. They pumped each other's hands like old friends united after a long separation. They could afford to laugh now that the danger was behind them.

Their refuge was a picture framer's shop. Along the walls were bins of unmounted work and others full of pictures, framed, wrapped, and ready to be called for. Samples of frames and the tools of the trade were neatly hung above them. A large worktable in the center of the room had been turned into a serving counter. There were dishes full of different kinds of fruit preserves, and they could hear something sizzling on a stove. Some of the travelers were already eating hungrily.

In the rear a short, red-faced woman stood over a coal stove making pancakes, flipping them onto a platter as they browned and pouring a new batch from her batter bowl as fast as she could. Even so, she could hardly accommodate the demand.

The guests, still arriving through the courtyard, ate as if they had never seen food before and didn't expect to soon again.

Karl refilled his plate over and over. Peter kept pace with him, taking time out to tell the cook they were the best pancakes he had ever eaten. They tried pancakes with lingonberries, pancakes with strawberry preserves, pancakes with cinnamon and sugar. When Karl had no appetite left, he took one more, rolled it up, and stuffed it into his coat pocket. Some of the others laughed at him, but it didn't worry him at all, and he noticed a few minutes later that even though they had made fun of him, lots of the others were following his example.

The last person to join them was a young man dressed in heavy corduroy slacks and a thick, hand-knitted fisherman's sweater. There was a sudden hush when he began to talk, and the fifteen people in the room listened to him attentively. He was their new instructor. His directions, like all they had been given, were minimal.

"Leave here two or three at a time, at intervals of ten or fifteen minutes. Cross the street and walk up to the square. On the other side of the square, beyond the street light—going east—hail the first cab you see. Ask to go to the Community Hospital, Emergency Entrance."

He repeated the directions in the identical words.

As soon as he stopped, he was bombarded with questions—some foolish, some frightened, others vital—for example: "Which way was east?" "What do your taxis look like?"

His answers were short and clear. When everyone seemed satisfied, he continued. "You will know when you are about to reach your destination. You drive along the canal for a good distance. It will be on your left. The hospital buildings will be on the right. You will pass them, and right afterwards the driver will make a right turn, then circle the block, coming back toward the canal on the street preceding the one he turned off on.

In other words, you will be facing the canal. The entrance to the emergency room will be on the left side of the street. Get out on that side, then cross the street, walk to the avenue bordering the canal, turn right at the corner, enter the first house, and go to the door at the top of the stairs."

The directions seemed impossibly involved, especially to the people who didn't know Copenhagen, of which Valby is a suburb. There were protests from many of the group that they would never remember them all. Some women were almost hysterical.

"I tell you what," the young man suggested. "I'll divide you into groups right now. One person in each group is bound to remember." He started doing the dividing himself. Karl and Peter stuck together. The man and woman grouped with them were still pleading for clearer instructions. Peter immediately assured them that Karl's memory was absolutely reliable. Calm returned. By the time the guide had slowly reviewed the directions once more, everyone seemed ready. He started out. Silently, and apparently confident now, the rest began to follow in groups at the proper intervals.

✿ 10 ✿
The Nurses' Residence

Karl had lived in Copenhagen with his sponsor when he first came to Denmark. She was the widow of a professor and still kept her apartment in the University district, near the center of the city. Her friends, as well as the museums and University gatherings she took him to, were all within a ten-minute trolley ride of her home.

He had never realized how far the outlying districts of Copenhagen were from the center of the city that borders the harbor and the network of canals branching off of it.

Their taxi ride from the picture-framing shop that night covered more than seven miles. The dank mist of early fall shrouded the quiet square of suburban Valby when they started out. But they were in no danger of missing their rendezvous. A taxi, as if forewarned, pulled up beside them before they could hail it. The precision of the complex machinery, operating anonymously to take them to safety, became more impressive at each step of their journey.

They got in behind the driver. Karl gave him their destination, as instructed. They were off, with the city almost to themselves.

For five minutes they rode in silence, expecting to see the canal at each turn and then to pull up at the hospital seconds later. They were traveling on narrow streets like the ones they had just left. They passed one city policeman on a corner. Now and then they saw another car making a crossing through the fog ahead. Once in the distance they heard the distinctive, blood-curdling sound of the ambulance siren. Gradually it faded in the distance, leaving nothing but the irregular pulse of the taxi engine running on its ersatz fuel. Ahead they heard the comforting clang of a trolley bell. It was all so familiar that Karl found himself thinking of his life so far behind in Düsseldorf.

They made another turn onto an extremely wide boulevard with trolley tracks in the middle. There were scarcely any buildings at all here. Instead of getting closer to the city, they seemed to be headed out to the country. Karl wanted to ask whether they had taken a wrong turn. As if anticipating his passengers' confusion, the driver turned around and began to describe the points of interest along the way.

They were passing the zoo. It was the oldest one in Scandinavia, he told them proudly, and you could spot its famous 144-foot tower rising above Valby Hill from almost any point in Copenhagen.

There were more fields beyond the zoo—the grounds

of Frederiksberg Castle. After that the city through which they were passing seemed more built up. They followed what looked like a main route north, turning right at the Assistens Churchyard onto another important artery.

Karl asked the driver why they were going by the most traveled route. The answer, when he heard it, seemed obvious. With so few cars abroad at night, those that traveled on out-of-the-way routes immediately roused suspicion and were stopped.

They must have been driving twenty-five minutes when Karl noticed that they were on an overpass. There seemed to be water underneath. They made the left turn he expected, after they had crossed it, and continued along what he supposed was the canal. The large buildings on the right, extending for several blocks, confirmed his first observation. They must belong to the hospital. A short block farther on, the driver turned right, then right again at the end of the block, and swung back at the next corner toward the canal. He pulled up on the left side near the corner. The hospital emergency entrance was visible, even in the dark. Karl got out and helped the others, then shut the door. When he tried to pay, his hand was pushed away. An almost imperceptible movement of the driver's head in the direction of the building across the way betrayed his concern for their safety. Karl tried to shake his hand, but he was off. Peter was already across the street. Hugging the buildings, he kept on around the corner, followed by their two companions. Karl came last.

The hallway behind the first door beyond the corner

was lighted by a tiny bulb. Karl didn't stop to look at the building's directory but headed straight for the stairs and took them two at a time.

He could hear the others ahead, walking lightly. They all reached the door on the fourth floor almost together. Peter pressed the bell. A gray-haired woman in nurse's uniform answered. The insignia on her cap indicated that she was the chief of the hospital's nursing staff. She motioned them in without speaking.

The apartment covered the entire floor. The building had been taken over recently to meet the need for quarters for the expanding nursing staff. The lower floors had been made into dormitories, but the apartment they were in had still not been converted. Presumably it had been reserved for the head nurse until it, too, would be needed for nurses' rooms. Probably few of the building's other inhabitants suspected the use it was being put to in the meantime.

In the living room off the hall, many of the group who had been at the pancake party had already settled down. There were others, too. The nurse showed Karl and Peter to a small bedroom beyond the kitchen. Two hospital cots, turned back and ready to go to sleep in, looked inviting after the long day. She opened the drawer of a large bureau and showed them clean clothes.

"I think they'll fit pretty well. There are trousers and jackets, too, in the closet. The bathroom is on the other side of the kitchen, down the hall. Change your clothes before you set out again."

After taking baths they dressed in the new clothes and went back to the living room. Some of the people who had been there when they came in had left. New people had arrived. But no one tried to be sociable. They were all as much in the dark about their destination as they had been from the beginning of their exodus. There was nothing to do but guess. Everyone was absorbed in his own imaginings. Karl put down the magazine he was trying to read. Peter stared into space. Karl caught his attention. They both got up and started for their room.

The nurse was in the kitchen when they walked through. "We'll wake you if it's necessary," she said, and wished them a good rest.

Karl woke up suddenly with the feeling that he had overslept. He shook Peter who was wound up in his covers like a snail in his shell. They could smell coffee and bacon and hear eggshells being cracked. Along with the clatter of plates and silver came the tinkle of girls' voices, chattering and laughing. There was something familiar in the sound. It was easy for a moment to imagine they were starting a leisurely vacation day.

When they left their room, they found a buffet set out on the dining-room table. Some of the "guests" were already eating. The boys helped themselves to hospital plates and cutlery and made their selection from the bacon, rolls, sweet breads, fish, and cheese set out for them.

Just as Karl came to the table, someone set down a platter of fresh scrambled eggs. He looked up to see who the waitress was and called: "Peter, come here." The girl giggled. Now he identified the familiar sound he'd heard from the bedroom.

Peter exclaimed: "Our schoolgirls!"

There was another giggle. It was Else, the blue-eyed, curly haired mimic whom they had seen in her school uniform, traveling with her classmates and teacher to see the Copenhagen museums and the castle at Elsinore. Instead of the navy blue school pinafore, she was now wearing the light blue chambray of a nurse in training, and her dark hair was pinned up—almost hidden—under her cap.

"How did *you* get here?" Karl asked, amazed.

"How did *you?*" she answered smartly.

One stupid question deserves another, Karl thought, as if she could answer any more than he could.

There was little anyone was free to talk about. It was surprising they made the effort to converse at all through the long wait that day.

The older people, for the most part, didn't. They were much too worried about the problem of survival and spent the time looking anxiously into the future or picking up one book or magazine after another, only to abandon it after a few minutes.

For the younger people, the nurses' residence might have been a resort hotel where they had met by chance. They cleaned up the kitchen together, then looked around for ways to amuse themselves. They started with cards. Before they had tired of solitaire, hearts, black jack, and old maid, some of the girls had made a survey of the food supplies and gotten permission to make candy. The fact that a shortage of sugar kept it from getting hard only added to the fun. They took turns eating it off the mixing spoon.

They couldn't sing. They couldn't dance for fear of

attracting attention with the noise. But the energy they lavished on arguing the merits of their favorite singers, jazz soloists, and songs was equaled only by the inexhaustible supply of riddles and guessing games they tried.

Players changed from time to time as some dropped out and spread themselves on the floor to read or look at magazines. But the games went on through lunch and into the afternoon.

Later a stranger joined them. By now they were experienced enough to suspect his arrival was a signal for their approaching departure.

He was there to give them directions, rather than to lead them himself. And, like the last guide, his instructions left the ultimate questions—when and how will we escape?—unanswered.

The next part of the journey sounded even more perilous and complicated than the taxi ride. And this time there was no driver to depend on. There was not even the reassuring prospect of a companion to bolster one's memory and moral courage. They would have to leave one at a time.

The stranger was patient. He did his best to clarify the instructions—even drawing the route and describing the landmarks for the more anxious. During all this Karl waited, restless. Neither he nor any of the other young people in the room would have voluntarily chosen to flee for their lives. But once the choice had been made for them, they were capable of enjoying the various episodes just as they had enjoyed the games that day. It would be time enough to worry about how to stay alive when someone held a gun at your chest. The possibility of dying was not even a consideration. They were all too young to realize it could happen to them.

The next step of their journey would coincide with the evening rush hour. With the streets and trolleys crowded, they would be less conspicuous, it was explained. They were told to get ready. Those who were hungry had coffee and sandwiches. The eager youngsters offered to go first, and the stranger singled out three or four of them—including Karl—to start off.

The stranger left first. A few minutes later others began to follow.

Karl was the third person. Saying, "See you soon," he waved airily to Peter and shut the door softly behind him. He went downstairs, all the way to the basement. Then he climbed a short flight of stone steps to a small door that gave onto an interior courtyard, crisscrossed with clotheslines full of sheets. Weaving between the white corridors they made, he found a door with a white mark near the bottom. He tried the handle. It was unlocked as he had been told it would be. He went down a second flight of stone steps like the ones he had just come out of, across the cellar to hall stairs leading up to the entrance. Then he opened the door ahead of him and walked out to find himself opposite the hospital's emergency entrance. If he waited, he wondered, would a fresh group of émigrés pull up and drop out of the same taxi he had arrived in the night before?

He did not stop to find out but walked at a normal pace down the street away from the canal. At the corner he turned left and went on a few blocks to the street where the trolley passed. Looking to the right, he could tell the stop by the line of people waiting at the curb. He joined them. The boy and girl who had left first were in the group, but before they heard the trolley bell in the distance, at least six more of his recent companions joined them. No sign of recognition passed among them.

When their trolley—Number 14—arrived, Karl got on with the rest, asked for a ticket "straight on," and found a place to stand back of the blackout curtain that screened off from the rest of the car the scant light the conductor needed for making change.

Everyone who got on would pass Karl where he stood, but the car was so full that he felt little danger of being noticed. Besides, the passengers, on entering, would be so absorbed in putting away their change, adjusting their bundles, and looking ahead for a seat that they would hardly have time to pay attention to him.

The only person he recognized in the small group standing around him was his friend with the "siren red" hair. It was still not dark enough—if it ever could be— to quench its flames.

Karl started to keep track of the stops. Then, if he failed to hear the conductor's call, he'd know where to get off anyhow. The car bobbed up and down, swaying rhythmically from side to side, as well. Karl could see no more of the passing scene than an occasional street sign when they stopped. The vibration of the wheels on the track made him sleepy. He pulled himself up short. He must not lose track of the stops—eleven, twelve. He started back through the car. The crowd had thinned out.

They had left the main part of the city behind. They

seemed to be entering a residential district. Mixed in
with small stores, there were many private houses with
lawns and gardens around them.

When his station was called, he was ready at the rear
door. He got off, mentally running through his instructions once more. The rest of his group got off, too. The
stop was a little safety island at the junction of two main
roads. On one side of the road was a cluster of shops.
On the other was the Tuborg brewery, big and dark and
Gothic in the gathering dusk. It was more like a medie-
val fortress than a beer works, in its parklike setting,
with wide entrances and heavy stone gateposts.

The fog that had been with them almost constantly
since Fynshav had lifted completely. The evening was
remarkably clear for October. Details of buildings and
the features of passers-by were sharp and distinct.

Karl would have welcomed a little fog at that moment. He didn't look forward to waiting for instructions
in this exposed spot. In a moment, however, his fears
were resolved. The little park was apparently a well-
established meeting place for the local community. A
few children ran up to meet their fathers, getting off the
same trolley. Older people, established on benches along
the sidewalk, were engaged in animated conversation
with their friends. Others were walking up and down, as
if in pursuit of their prescribed daily quota of exercise
and fresh air. There was a children's corner, where a
group of boys and girls almost his own age were laughing and talking around a girls' jacks contest.

The activity and life of the little triangle was so varied

that Karl felt the members of their group would hardly be noticed walking around one by one among the regular inhabitants. As he joined the rest of the promenaders, he saw the stranger he was expecting on a bench at the tip end of the triangle.

Karl watched the trolleys as they continued to arrive. Three came and went. Peter was not on any of them.

Some of the group had already left. Karl had seen the stranger dispatch them. Now and then one member of the group would stop, as if to exchange greetings with him for a moment, and then resume his walk. A few moments later that person would be missing from the triangle.

Karl continued to walk alone. One person after another from his group departed. As darkness fell, the other regular visitors were leaving the park, too. He was beginning to wonder whether he had been forgotten when he heard a voice behind him say, "Excuse me."

The stranger had left the bench and followed him. He walked ahead now—just a step or two—and, as if talking to himself, said softly, but with perfect clarity: "You are next. Go through the brewery gate and keep to the right. If anyone comes toward you from the other direction, stay on the walk. In Denmark we always keep to the right. If you step off, you will be turned back. Understand? You will come to a man standing in a doorway with an unlighted cigarette in his mouth. You say: 'Pardon me, can you tell me where to find the shipping manager?' "

Then the stranger was gone. Karl continued walking

to the other side of the triangle, crossed the wide street, and headed toward the huge stone markers bordering the entrance to the brewery.

He heard another trolley approach and grind to a clattering stop as he walked through the gateway. He dared not look back to see if Peter had come.

The driveway with its narrow sidewalks on each side wound around the imposing main building, towering and black in the gathering dark. Karl took the right-hand walk. With the drive on his left and the blank brick wall of a building on his right, he had barely room to stay on the path. The more carefully he walked, the harder it seemed to be to keep his balance. He continued for the longest quarter of a mile he had ever known before he saw a shack ahead. Coming closer, he made out a man in the doorway. A cap was pulled down on his face. An unlighted cigarette hung from the corner of his mouth. He was absolutely expressionless. Karl stopped. The man seemed to take no notice of him.

"Pardon me," Karl began. "Can you tell me where to find the shipping manager?"

"My friend," the man answered quickly, "I will. Follow the path right and then left." He gestured behind him to point the way. "And repeat your question to the next man."

Then he paused as if to emphasize his next words. "Thirty-five—and you are the last one."

The man's relief was obvious. But to Karl, his words were like a death sentence. "The last one." That meant that Peter had not made it. What had happened? What could he do? Now there was not even time to think.

There was no time for anything except concentrating on the question he must ask again. Ahead of him, standing against a shack even more ramshackle than the one he had just passed, he could already see the next man.

He began to repeat the question to him. "Pardon me. Can you tell—" Before he could finish, he was pushed through the door. He tripped, landing in someone's lap.

He was in a crowded unlighted hut. A voice whispered: "That's all." For a minute in the darkness, he was left to wonder into whose hands he had fallen. Then a voice he did not recognize began:

"You will go through the door I shall open, one at a time. You will be on a narrow dock. You will see a small boat directly ahead of you. Make a dash for it and throw yourself into the hold. Remember, jump! There is no time to climb in. A searchlight scans this spot every twenty seconds. Each person will leave the moment the beam crosses the threshold. He must be under cover in the boat before it completes its revolution. I will give each of you the starting signal."

He repeated the instructions again. There was a breathless pause. The man crossed the hut, picking his way among the tightly packed people on the floor. The searchlight crossed a small slit in the wallboards. The door handle turned. The light circled again. The door opened. A body darted out. The door shut. The light came closer. The door opened a crack. The light passed. Someone else dashed out.

There were no other sounds. Karl's turn was getting closer. A woman's voice next to him cried: "I can't. I'm afraid to jump. I can't."

"Shh. Follow me. I'll catch you." Karl grabbed her hand and edged toward the door.

He landed like one more sea bass on top of those who had gone before him in the hold of a small fishing vessel. There was barely time to brace himself before the woman dropped into his arms as he had told her to.

Thirty-five people were in a space that might have accommodated ten comfortably. Comfortably, that is, if you could ignore the fact that, where they were, fish had been first. Stuffed in, as they were, like a big catch, and covered with a tarpaulin, comfort was out of the question.

A sailor above tied down the canvas. Apparently satisfied that nothing looked out of the ordinary, the captain started the engine. They were moving.

✿ 11 ✿

Under Way

The group had changed. Mothers with small children and babies in arms had joined the fifteen who had been together in Copenhagen. The boat rode as smoothly as an automobile on a well-paved highway, but nothing could offset the effects of the foul air under the tarpaulin.

Only the children seemed impervious to it. Most of them had fallen asleep before the boat took off. All of them were unnaturally quiet. Karl soon learned why. A woman whose baby he held for a moment explained that they had been doped for fear their crying might attract unwelcome attention.

People were sick. An old woman who had been separated from her husband and feared that they would never find each other moaned fitfully. But these sounds were drowned out by the racket of the motor. A person on deck would never have guessed what a strange cargo was in the hold.

Karl was beginning to relax when the baby next to him started to whimper. He was no expert in child care, but he had seen and heard enough babies to know they don't give up easily when they're hungry. The child was wiggling and kicking in its mother's arms. The fussing was changing to purposeful yells. The mother rocked it and patted it and cooed, with no effect. It was crying angrily enough now to be heard all the way to Berlin, Karl thought. The other passengers told the mother to keep the baby quiet, as if she could press a button. "Feed it," a man urged.

"I have nothing," the mother answered. "They said he would stay asleep."

"He'll wake my baby," another mother said. "Then what will we do?"

"Supposing someone hears him?" It was a man's voice again. The thought chilled them all.

On the other side of Karl, another man said quietly: "Let me have him. I'm a doctor." He moved closer to the mother and took the screaming child. He put him over his knees and pulled something from his pocket. Then he asked Karl to uncover the baby's leg and hold it still. There was one howl as the doctor's needle punctured the baby's buttock, then immediate silence. Karl gave the baby back to his mother. She was crying herself, now.

"He'll be all right, I'm sure. Don't worry. But there better be a bottle for him when he wakes up again," the doctor said.

They had barely settled down after this episode when

a sudden silence descended. The motor was dead. They heard another boat drawing closer. It came alongside. A voice with a German accent called: "Who are you? What's your business? Where are you bound?"

The captain answered easily, as if they were old friends. "Hello. How are you?" Then he gave the registration number of the boat. "We're making for the port tonight. Fishing's been good. We've got a full hold."

"From Hven—wasn't it?" the German asked.

"Yes, Hven," the captain replied steadily.

"Good trip. Go ahead," the German answered. His boat's motor picked up. He pulled away.

Still not a sound in the hold. Not even a breath was drawn. No sound on deck either.

Then the motor started feebly, sputtered, and died. You could hear the lap of water on the hull, it was so quiet. A second time the engine sputtered as if to die again; then it caught at the last moment, choked, and began to smooth out into an even chuga, chuga, chug, chug, chug—the most comforting sound Karl had ever heard. The captain threw it into gear, and with a loud groan it began to pull. Once more they were off.

The captain's success produced a strange kind of gaiety in the cramped quarters below deck. The young people began to speculate in whispers about where they would land. When the old woman began to cry again, one of the girls said: "Now, now. If it's as easy as this, you don't have to fear for your husband. Cheer up." And she did.

It seemed no time before the tarpaulin was thrown

back and the captain was looking down at them. "We're safe now. Stay where you are, but at least we can give you some air. Just cover up fast if I say so."

The moon was out. The riffles of the wake glistened in the silver light. Everywhere else the water was quiet as a pond. There was not a trace of mist. Every object as far as the eye could reach was perfectly limned against the horizon. Behind them the German patrol boat was almost lost in the distance. The shore was fast receding. Ahead, a few fishing boats trawled back and forth or rested at anchor. They must have been familiar. Their captain took no notice. He seemed to be concentrating on something off the port bow. In a moment he pointed. At first Karl saw nothing, but he kept his eyes in that direction, straining to pierce the night. Only two or three others were sitting high enough to see over the gunwales. One of them gasped. Almost at that instant Karl saw—small, low, still indistinct—something that might be an island.

"It's Swedish soil. It's Hven. We'll be there within the hour," the captain told them.

To Karl, Hven was no more than a name. He had no idea of whether it was north or south, near or far from the mainland of Sweden. Nor was he interested. At that moment it was enough to know that safety was in sight.

They landed at a dock even smaller than the one they had embarked from. A man in an unfamiliar uniform was waiting for them. They tried to pay the captain for their trip, but their offers were turned aside. "It's all been arranged," was all the explanation they got. Karl and the other young people had nothing left but small change. They forced it on the two crewmen. "After all," Karl told them, "we can't use it here. We're not paying you. We're trying to keep our good Danish money from being wasted."

One of the boys found a mop. Someone else discovered a brush and sponges. They all pitched in, over the protests of captain and crew, and fifteen minutes later they had cleaned the boat so thoroughly that even its ancestral aroma of fish was almost destroyed.

Before they had finished, the uniformed man who had taken off the women and children was back for them. They shook hands with the captain and his men and said good-by. "God grant we'll all be back home together soon," the captain said.

They were taken to a house that seemed to be a small inn for sailors. The rest of the group were in the dining room already enjoying what seemed to be a tremendous meal. Else caught his eye. "I've saved a place. Sit here."

Her first thought was for Peter. She had no more idea of what could have happened than Karl did. She had left the nurses' residence soon after him. The elderly woman followed her. It seemed to her that the nurse was purposely spacing the younger people between the more fearful to give them courage. She had expected Peter would follow the woman.

"He couldn't have been caught," Karl said.

"Of course not," Else agreed, but she sounded no more sure than Karl.

"Maybe we'll find him at the next stop. Have you found out what it is?" he asked.

A man from the Swedish Red Cross had talked to the

group in the hotel while the boys were cleaning the boat. He said they would be leaving as soon as they had eaten and rested. It was only a short boat ride to the mainland. They were going to a kind of temporary barracks until government aides could place them properly for their stay in Sweden.

"We were told not to talk about how we got here—not to anyone. The man was very emphatic about that," Else said at the end.

"I can understand. We might give away some of the escape routes to the wrong people."

"Do you know how we got here? It's incredible. The whole thing was planned from the Copenhagen Resistance headquarters: every move each of us made from the start. The boy next to me on the boat wasn't Jewish. He had been a Resistance messenger. The leaders thought the Nazis suspected him, so the underground wanted him out of Denmark before he was caught. He didn't tell me how *he* got on the boat."

"He's probably seen enough evidence of what can happen when secrets leak."

The room was warm. The schnapps that they had been drinking was taking effect. The company began to sing. The older children were beginning to wake up. A little girl with blond curls started to dance in time to their music—all by herself. Even those who were preoccupied smiled at the good spirits of the rest.

After the last of the meal was cleared away, some people stretched out on chairs and couches, but the boys and girls and many of the children went on singing and dancing until it was time to leave.

They were in the midst of a dance when they were told to get ready. All of them—led by Karl and Else—kept on singing and dancing, out through the lobby down the winding road to the boat. The sky was already beginning to lighten in the east. They had been up all night.

✸ 12 ✸
Out of the Blizzard

They landed at Hälsingborg on the Swedish mainland in broad daylight, were ushered to a waiting truck, and after a fifteen-minute ride drove up to a modern cement-and-glass building in the midst of rolling acres of grass and trees. Under the Red Cross banner tacked above the entrance, the name of a girls' boarding school was chiseled in the lintel stone.

The broad wooden doors were open wide. They walked in, past a counter where books, magazines, candy, and cigarettes were sold, to a large bare room that looked as if it might have been the study hall. At the far end more than a score of women and children clustered together, peering anxiously at the newcomers as they entered the room.

"Daddy, Daddy," a child's voice cried. A boy of five or six, jumping up and down with excitement, tried to break away from his mother.

Next to Karl, the man with the dyed red hair stopped in his tracks, then turned abruptly and hurried back the way he had come. The little boy began to sob. His mother held him close, trying to comfort him, but he broke loose, screaming "Daddy, Daddy," over and over.

As Karl looked to see what had possessed the father to turn back in sight of his family, the man pushed past him and elbowed his way ahead. The child's face was at once magically transformed. The man reached him and held him high. Now the little boy was giggling with the tears still running down his face. His mother was smiling and crying, too. The father had gone back for candy, and now he was emptying his pockets and stuffing bar after bar of chocolate into his son's small hands. The little boy couldn't hold them all. At first he tried to pick up the ones he dropped, but they were coming too fast. Bars of chocolate fell all around him. The whole family was laughing as if they couldn't stop. The father hugged the mother. The child's voice sounded loud and clear. "Where did you get that hair? It looks funny."

Laughter broke out all over the room where, like Karl, people had stopped in their tracks to watch. Then the movement toward the waiting women and children resumed. Peter was not there.

During the next days they were settled in dormitories, supplied with clothes and toilet articles, and instructed in the customs of the country. Records were made of their background, education, special training, and work experience. They were interviewed about their likes and dislikes in food, people, climate, sports, and so on.

When they were not being interviewed or tested, they played games and read. Sometimes they walked to town and explored the stores—although they had no money to spend—or visited the library or the museum. A great deal of the time Karl and Else looked for clues to Peter's whereabouts. They questioned everyone, in case someone might have seen Peter at some stage in his journey. Each morning they joined the group searching the faces of the new arrivals as they came into the big hall of the reception center, until the performance had become a ritual whose purpose they had almost forgotten. They found no trace of their friend.

By the end of their second week of internment, the camp was a rumor factory. Karl's situation was not unique. There were a dozen or more others waiting, like him, for someone who had not come. Each group produced different stories. An overloaded customs boat had swamped. The twenty refugees aboard were lost. One group's guide had betrayed them. Some of the party managed to escape, but most of them were caught when they were already in sight of their rescue boat.

Karl could imagine Peter in each of the catastrophes he heard about. He didn't want to hear any more. He began to stay by himself more and more. One day when he was in his room alone, reading, the director sent for him and told him they had found a place for him with a farm family in the north.

He knew Karl preferred city life and work as a carpenter or cabinetmaker. But he urged him to go north rather than wait any longer. "I can guarantee it's a family you'll like, and they'll keep you busy. That counts for a lot when you're worried and alone."

Karl didn't know how to refuse. "I would go tomorrow," he said, "but I was hoping my friend would come before I left."

The director anticipated his reaction. "We knew that would be a problem. But I think we can arrange it so he'll be sure to get in touch with you. We know his name and what he looks like. We'll tell him where you are and have him wire you as soon as he arrives."

It seemed reasonable, and Karl agreed to go. But later, thinking it over, he felt uneasy. How did he know that Peter wasn't in Sweden already? He could have come through another port. Karl explained his concern to the director and asked him whether there was any central place where every Dane in Sweden was registered. While the director didn't hold out much hope that Peter might have come by another route, he referred Karl to the Danish consul. The consul sent him on to a Swedish newspaper editor who ran many ads for people searching for lost relatives.

It was too late to visit the newspaper, which was in Göteborg, a little farther north. Instead, Karl prepared a public notice addressed to Peter in which he told him to write or call and gave him his new address and phone number. The clerk at the consulate lent him money to pay for inserting it in the paper. He sent it with a note, asking the editor to continue the ad until further notice and send the bills to him.

The next morning he said good-by to Else, who was

still waiting for a place in a family where she could help the mother with the children and the housework. Each of them promised to get in touch with the other at once if there was any news of Peter.

The north of Sweden in the shortening days of fall was a cheerless place. In the few daylight hours, the sky seemed already heavy with the snow that would fall all winter. The mountains shaded the valleys and appeared to close one in. It was a more rugged land by far than even the windswept farm in Jutland where Karl had made his first home in Scandinavia.

He was prepared to become a farmer again. But at the end of the first week at the Holmgrens' in a small village northwest of Uppsala, he suspected that he had been invited to stay there because they wanted to help him, not because they needed a farm hand. There wasn't much to do. Mr. Holmgren seemed to have more than enough help already, with two sturdy boys who did their chores before they went to school in the morning and after they came home at night.

Karl tried to pitch in, but they wouldn't let him. He asked Mr. Holmgren if he couldn't find something to do in the village, but the farmer insisted they needed him at home. Every week he paid Karl the small salary they had agreed upon. Every week Karl sent most of it off to the paper to keep the notice for Peter running.

The snow began to fall. Snowshoes were taken down from the barn wall where they hung. With the boys' help, Karl made a pair for himself. They turned out so well that Mr. Holmgren encouraged him to set up a small workshop in a corner of the barn. His first work was a large dining-room table for the Holmgrens. Things were hard to buy because of the war, and the family, with two boys and two girls, had grown far beyond the furniture they had started housekeeping with fifteen years before.

One night Mr. Holmgren joined Karl in the barn. He tossed the weekly bill from the newspaper onto the workbench and sat down with his evening pipe to watch Karl. They talked about the table, and Karl described the kind of chairs he'd like to make to go with it. Then Mr. Holmgren changed the subject abruptly. "Karl, you're going to need some more clothes."

Karl looked down at the heavy corduroy pants he wore every day. He kept the woolen ones he had been given for special occasions. "These look as if they'd last a while," he said. Mr. Holmgren chose not to answer Karl's remark.

"And you should be putting something aside to get you started after the war is over. You could stay here, but I know you prefer Denmark."

"I'll get a job then. That's no problem." Karl couldn't see that far ahead.

"But it could be. There'll be chaos when the war is over, until things are straightened out. You can't depend on getting a job at all. I don't know how to put it, Karl. I know it's hard, but if Peter hasn't gotten here yet, I'm afraid he's not coming. Why don't you stop running that ad?"

The truth Karl had been trying to escape was suddenly unavoidable. Mr. Holmgren was right. It was as if he had known it all along. He kept on sanding the table leg he was working on. Without stopping or even looking up, he said: "All right, Mr. Holmgren. I'll do that. I guess you're right."

The next day he sent off a letter to the editor enclosing the money for a last ad. "I can no longer afford the notice," he wrote. "And it seems foolish, after so long, to hope that my friend will make it to Sweden."

There was an answer by return mail. It said: "You can run the ad as long as you like. Don't worry about the money. We want to help if we can."

Karl showed it to Mr. Holmgren. He read it, then, smiling, turned to Karl. "Well, I'm glad you've finally found a good Swede."

"There're bound to be one or two good people in any country," Karl joked back.

Karl wrote and thanked the editor at once, but he no longer hoped. He worked as hard as he could to try to forget Denmark, just as he had learned, long ago, to forget about home.

The table he made for his hosts was so successful that he went on with the chairs. Before they were finished, some friends of the Holmgrens asked him to make a chest for them. He began to spend most of the day at the workbench. When he offered to clean the barn or feed the cattle, the older man urged him to go back to his work. "I'll ask you to help when I need you. Meantime, keep on with your furniture. You'll be supporting us all at this rate."

Early in November Else wrote that she was settled with a doctor's family in Stockholm. They began to write each other regularly. There were many Danes in the city, she said, and regular meetings and social gatherings given by the consulate or by one of the Swedish families like hers that had a refugee living with them. Else described the gatherings in exact detail—the food, the people, the entertainment. But whatever gaiety she conveyed was always canceled by the ending of her letters. "I asked about Peter, but no one knew anything."

It was plain that she was just as homesick in the city—in spite of movies, museums, parties, and fellow countrymen—as he was alone on the Holmgrens' farm. It was natural. She was a Dane. Until the day her headmistress had told her that she must leave the country immediately, she had never known what it was to be set apart from her friends as Karl had been in Germany. She had never lived, as Jews all over Europe had for centuries, with the ever-present threat of sudden, unexplained attack. Without warning, her secure foundation had been torn away. Her parents and brothers and sisters, who might have given her comfort, had vanished as finally as Peter had. She had said good-by on the station platform and waved from her compartment in the train when she went off to school in September. She had received and sent the usual letters and never said good-by.

When Karl told the Holmgrens the news about Else, Mrs. Holmgren asked him if he'd like to invite her for the holidays, thinking it might lift both their spirits. And indeed it did. As soon as Else wrote that she would come, he began to look forward again, for the first time since he'd come to Sweden.

In the Holmgren household, preparations for the

holiday began in mid-November. Mrs. Holmgren was already laying away fruit cakes soaked in brandy. When Karl came in from the barn in the late afternoons, the kitchen was heavy with the scent of cinnamon and anise and ginger. The tables were covered to the last inch with cookies shaped like horns, and bells, birds, and angels; with cookies cut in squares or delicately etched with stars and flowers and crescents, all laid out to cool and crisp before storing.

The children were constantly darting back and forth on secret missions. Each one had a personal hiding place for the mysterious presents he was working on in private, whenever there was a moment free. Mealtimes were lively with plans for decorations and ornaments and parties and games. The spirit of celebration was contagious.

Karl had sent Else directions and told her which train they would meet. But, a week before her arrival, when he had no idea he would hear from her again, Mrs. Holmgren ran out to his shop before lunch one day with a letter from her.

"Let's hope she hasn't changed her plans," Mrs. Holmgren said as she handed it to Karl.

Karl hoped not, too. He opened it hurriedly. Almost immediately he let out a shout of joy, threw the letter away, and caught Mrs. Holmgren in an embrace that almost strangled her.

"She's found Peter, I think! Read it! Quick! Read it." He picked up the letter, gave it to Mrs. Holmgren, then ran out into the barn calling Mr. Holmgren. "Come here! Read this! It's about Peter!"

They read it over together. Karl was calmer now. The Holmgrens didn't speak at first.

"It doesn't say he's actually been found, does it? But if someone thinks Peter was on the crossing with them from Gilleleje and it gives the date, he must be in Sweden somewhere."

Mr. Holmgren didn't want to dash Karl's hopes. On the other hand, he didn't want to encourage him for nothing. "It's certainly more hopeful than anything you've heard so far. Let's follow it up."

Without stopping to change the boots he'd been wearing to clean the cow stalls, he started toward the house. Mrs. Holmgren left her baking, and with Karl they both started planning a search. By midafternoon they had written a dozen letters, which Karl took into town and posted special delivery.

They wrote to the Red Cross in Hven, in Hälsingborg, and in the other major cities; to the Danish consulates in Hälsingborg and in every other city that seemed large enough to have a Danish representative. They wrote, too, to the leaders of the Jewish communities in all the leading cities.

The letters described Peter, reported that he might have traveled from Gilleleje on November 2, and asked for the kindness of an immediate reply, telling whether or not they had any news and, if so, giving details. The letters closed: "If you are in contact with him now, please ask him to wire collect immediately."

The next days were hard to endure. Then letters began to arrive, the first from the Red Cross. They wrote that they were forbidden to give out information about any client without his authorization. Karl could only hope that Peter was a client, and if he was, that the Red Cross would tell him about Karl's letter and ask him to authorize sending his address to Karl. He wrote back at once and asked if they would please convey his message to Peter if they knew where he was. He sent copies of this second letter to the other Red Cross offices he had written to in the first place, but he was not optimistic about the outcome.

Day after day frustrating letters like the first kept coming from branch offices of the Red Cross all over Sweden. It was not even necessary to finish the notes from Danish consulates in Hven, in Hälsingborg, in Stockholm, beginning: "Sorry to disappoint you."

The most discouraging word was from Landskrona. "There was a Peter on a boat from Gilleleje, just before the date you mention. But he was not German, and his last name was Wölby."

Karl could not pretend to hide his disappointment after that letter had come. And the Holmgrens could not pretend they did not share it. That night even the children were subdued. For days they had been enlisting Karl's help. He had given them ideas for carved ornaments for the tree, showed them how to use the carving blades, and made what they considered the most beautiful ones himself. He had supervised their painting and decorating, which the girls worked on, by his side, at the big table after dinner.

Tonight there was not even a mention of Christmas. Mrs. Holmgren began to play carols, and the children with their father dutifully tried to sing, but the messages of joy and good spirits were out of key. After one or two songs, the carolers went off one at a time, and Mrs. Holmgren gave up playing and sat down with her knitting.

The children went to bed. For some time Karl sat motionless, holding his knife in one hand, a half-finished ornament in the other, looking into the fire. Mr. Holmgren got up and began putting out the lights. He looked out the window. "It's still snowing," he reported. "It looks like the biggest fall of this season. I can't even see the road, it's so thick."

"When Else arrives, we'll go for her in the sleigh, Karl. She'll enjoy that, I bet."

Karl didn't answer. Instead, he quietly put down his work and got up. Without looking at either of his hosts, he quietly said good night and went upstairs. They had never seen him so sad.

⁕ 13 ⁕

A Last-Minute Present

Mrs. Holmgren waited with some apprehension for Karl to come down for breakfast the next morning, but he was his usual cheerful self. The children greeted him with the announcement that they were going to teach him to ski as soon as their chores were done. They were already waxing their boards in front of the fireplace. Karl made each child tell him what kind of skier he was. Then he promised to make new skis for the one who looked best to him going cross-country that morning.

He talked to Mr. Holmgren about cleaning up the sleigh and getting it ready to fetch Else that afternoon. Where the plow had been through, there were banks of snow higher than a man's head on either side of the highway.

The girls and their mother were still worrying about last-minute plans for the annual Christmas Eve party, to which all the relatives and friends for miles around would be coming the next night. Karl offered to set up the tables and even to butter bread. It was as if he were trying to make amends for his glumness of the night before.

"Else will enjoy your Christmas more than anyone," he said. "She loves celebrations."

The children scarcely took time for breakfast. They left their plates half empty, their chocolate in their cups, and rushed off so they could get their work done and start out on their skis.

Karl followed them to the barn and worked on the sleigh.

Mrs. Holmgren started to clear the table. She put some dishes down beside the sink, then paused for a minute, looking out the window. "He's a wonderful boy," she said to her husband. "He's heartbroken about Peter, and look at him."

"He's determined not to let it spoil our Christmas, isn't he?" her husband replied. "I'd give anything if his could be happy."

Mr. Holmgren went out. A little later she watched him plowing the barnyard and driveway with Karl. Before she had finished straightening up downstairs, she heard the sleigh bells and the children singing. Karl had harnessed up for a trial run. He was driving. Beside him and behind him were the Holmgren children and half a dozen neighbors—all holding their skis in their arms and singing Christmas carols at the top of their lungs. Karl was singing with them, flicking the dappled gray lightly with his long whip to spur her on, looking

as gay as the merry little girl—the Holmgrens' youngest—who was standing beside him, with both arms
tightly clasped around his neck for support.

Two hours later they were all back again, warming
their hands and stocking feet in front of the fire—so
hungry that they were already stealing bread from the
luncheon table to munch on while they compared per-
formances on the morning runs.

Karl had awarded the skis to his favorite—the youngest. He claimed she was fastest, considering the length
of her legs. He was determined to have the prize ready
for Christmas and was busy taking measurements. The
older boys teased him, saying they'd never be ready,
but Karl insisted they'd be ready enough to look like skis.
He could put on the finishing touches later.

Mr. Holmgren pointed out some mail for him on the
hall table when he came in for lunch. Karl paid no attention, but after lunch, when everyone else was occupied,
he casually opened the letters, read them where he was
standing, and dropped them again without bothering to
replace them in their envelopes. No one asked any questions. Mr. Holmgren, who had looked up from his paper
to watch Karl's response, went back to his reading to
avoid catching the young man's eye. Karl put on his
jacket, called over his shoulder, "I'm going to work on
those skis," and went out without coming back to the
living room. One of the boys ran after him and called
from the door: "You forgot the measurements." Karl took
the paper from his hand sheepishly and turned back to
his workshop.

Before he returned to the house to get ready to go for
Else, Mrs. Holmgren had put the letters out of sight. She

didn't need to read them to know they had nothing to say. She prayed that the next week would be so busy that Karl would have little time for thinking. She was glad Else was coming. That would help.

The sun had already completed its brief winter visit for the day before the family had bundled up and started out for the afternoon train. It was Mr. Holmgren's idea that everyone should go, and it was an inspired one. Else's face was radiant as she jumped off the train into Karl's hug and caught sight of the sleigh full of parents and children shouting Merry Christmas, and dogs barking their greeting.

The boys took her luggage, tossing the suitcases under the seat. Karl helped her up beside him on the driver's seat, and they started off in the starry night.

She and Karl didn't even have a chance to ask each other how they were before the children began bombarding her with news. They had to report on the day's skiing and ask if she knew how. They had to inquire about Stockholm and get descriptions of each of the children in the family she lived with. They had to catch her up on the Christmas preparations and tell her about their friends. When they started singing, she had a chance for the inevitable questions about Peter.

"I think it's hopeless. We ought to try to forget," Karl told her.

Her eyes filled, and she looked earnestly at Karl. "We can't. That isn't fair, Karl. We can't give up already."

Karl didn't say any more. For a moment he covered her hands, clutched together under the blanket, in his own big mittened one. Then he joined in the singing.

Mrs. Holmgren had watched it all. Before they had

reached the farm, she was full of schemes to interest, amuse, occupy, and distract both Else and Karl, but she never needed them. The children were so delighted with Else—with her curly black hair and blue eyes, so unfamiliar to them, and with the dance steps she brought from Copenhagen and the guessing games she knew— and she was so excited by the signs of festivity wherever she turned and so eager to add touches of her own that there wasn't an empty or silent moment.

That night the little girls helped her unpack and change to country clothes. Then when the table was set, they stuck apples with cloves and bits of cinnamon bark and roasted them to eat with hot wine before supper. Finally, there was the great meal itself—a prelude to the real Christmas feast that would follow.

By the time Else had helped Mrs. Holmgren put away the last of the silver and glasses, the younger children had tired of their games and singing and crept off to bed, unasked. Karl came in from working on the skis.

"You can't be washing dishes *still!*" he joked. "I could have been finished long ago."

"And so would the dishes," Else teased back. "You do the eating, and we'll take care of the rest."

The next day began earlier and was even busier than the one before. Else started to help clean up after breakfast, but Mrs. Holmgren begged her to go with the others to get the Christmas tree.

Karl coaxed her, too. "This is one thing you've never done before. In Denmark you need a magnifying glass to find a Christmas tree."

It was an errand they might have completed in min-

utes, but they gave it hours. The meadows were all bordered with evergreens—any one of which would have been perfect—but the purpose of the expedition would have been lost if they had cut one of those. They went from hill to farther hill. No sooner had one of the children sighted a tree that he liked than another would veto it, claiming it had a crooked trunk or a misshapen limb, that it was too stubby or too big or too scrawny or too full. The most insignificant flaw was enough to rule out a prospective candidate for the honor of gracing the Holmgren living room. A word of complaint from anyone and the whole band would set off on the search again until someone called. Then the whole sequence of inspection, appraisal, and rejection was repeated.

It was understood that Mr. Holmgren would make the final decision. His choice was usually dictated more by the temperature of his fingers and toes and the hours of elapsed time since the start of the search than by the measurable superiority of his selection.

When he first said: "This is it," there were torrents of protest. Each of the children insisted now that any one of dozens they had turned down would do twice as well. He told them they could take any other in sight that they could all agree was preferable. All four of them ran wildly back and forth, looking, sizing up, and comparing their father's tree with the rejected ones. Finally, everyone, including Karl, Else, and Mr. Holmgren, agreed on a heavy spruce of delicate blue-green. They agreed that the undeniable bare spot on one side could be hidden when the tree was arranged in the traditional corner of the living room.

The baby of the family, Karl's favorite, piped up: "Maybe no one else will want it. Let's take it so it will be happy on Christmas."

Karl couldn't resist gathering her up and hugging her for this. Everyone laughed affectionately. She was so sweet and earnest.

The biggest boy cut the tree with two clean strokes of his ax and started off with it down the hill toward home. Karl gave the smallest child a ride on his shoulders. She bounced gaily, waving a miniature tree he had cut off with his pocket knife especially for her.

Back home, they decorated the house and trimmed the tree while Mrs. Holmgren got the ham ready for the oven and went on with other preparations for the party meal.

The smell of thyme and basil and ginger and cloves began to float through the house as the ham started cooking and the traditional lutfisk simmered on the stove. The little girls finished their strings of berries and straw flowers and wreathed the tree from top to bottom.

Else picked up after them as she might have done at home. At one point, Karl and the oldest boy brought in a mysterious bundle wrapped in burlap and made elaborate efforts to secrete it in the corner of the dark coat closet —as if no one had a clue that it was the Christmas skis.

At lunchtime Mrs. Holmgren put a big plate of cheese, a basket of black bread, a pitcher of milk, and four or five kinds of thinly sliced sausage on the table. "This is all you get," she announced, as if she were starving them. "If we don't hurry, our guests will be here before we've finished."

Everyone was too excited to be very hungry. Besides, they'd been sampling the meal from the moment they had come back with the tree. They ate as many nuts as they cracked. They nibbled on raisins, tried the cookies fresh from the oven, grabbed the crusts cut from the sandwich bread, and took lickings of the endless assortment of fillings she was spreading on open sandwiches.

She knew what she was saying when she prodded them. Else was still braiding the little one's shiny blond hair when they heard the first sleigh in the drive. Before they could get downstairs, Mr. Holmgren was greeting the guests at the door. The party had begun.

Mr. Holmgren lighted the candles on the tree and in the towering candelabrum on the mantel. The boys built up the fire in the fireplace to a roaring blaze. Now the guests were arriving, two and three families at a time. Someone was playing for a little group of carolers at the piano. The girls were passing the trays of sandwiches and glass cups full of punch. Mr. Holmgren was pouring aquavit for the men, who were lighting up their pipes and warming their hands, cold from holding the reins through the long sleigh rides.

For hours they ate and drank and sang. Some of the older children got out violins they had brought and, at their parents' coaxing, played their well-prepared solos or their favorite carols. There were chorales with recorders. There were games for the little children— passing the penny, blindman's buff, musical chairs. Then Else suggested dancing. She ran upstairs to get records she had brought, cleared a corner near the dining room, turned on the phonograph, and began to

teach the young people—using Karl and the Holmgren children to demonstrate new steps.

When Mrs. Holmgren finally clapped her hands and announced the *real* dinner, the house was ringing with music and laughter. Somehow, amidst the hubbub, little tables had been set up around the living room and arranged for the children. The grownups were to sit together at the large dining-room table.

Mrs. Holmgren said: "Are we ready?"

Silence fell at once. Mr. Holmgren's strong bass gave the pitch, and young and old joined in "Now It's Christmas Again," a favorite Swedish carol. When it was over, all heads bowed in prayer. Mr. Holmgren spoke: "For all that we have been given, for all that we have been forgiven, we thank Thee God. We thank Thee on this night, especially, for the Miracle of Christ that is renewed each year, bringing to us all—however young, however old—the message of peace and human brotherhood which, we pray, may some day guide all men—wherever, whoever, whatever they may be."

There was a pause. "Bless especially the young people who are strangers here tonight and grant that they may soon be restored to their families and friends to live as Christ taught His followers—circled in love and guided by charity."

The chatter and laughter picked up as quickly as it had stopped. Three of the children rushed to help Else and Karl to their tables, while the youngest ran in and out among the grownups, trying to guide them to their places. Since she had made all the place cards herself, she knew where each guest belonged.

Mr. Holmgren had begun to carve the ham, given the place of honor on the sideboard, surrounded by a tureen of flaky lutfisk in snowy mustard-flavored cream sauce, trays of herring in every form imaginable, and a long dish of spiced spare ribs. The first plate had just been passed when the party was interrupted by insistent pounding on the front door. One of the boys got up to go, but before he could reach the hall, the handle rattled and a voice called: "Can someone give me money for the taxi?"

Karl and Else rushed from their places, dropping their napkins behind them. Else was laughing hysterically.

"Peter, it's you. I don't believe it," Karl shouted, and while everyone gathered around to share the excitement, the two friends met in the doorway and locked in a bear hug.

It was only when Else caught his attention that Peter would finally let go of Karl. She cried unashamedly as he pulled her to him. Mrs. Holmgren, as usual, saved the day. She stood next to Karl. "It's my turn, Peter," she said. "We've been waiting for you *almost* as anxiously as Karl and Else have. Introduce us, Karl, won't you?"

And Karl did. He took Peter's hand and Else took the other, and before he could even take off his coat and boots, they led him all around the party, introducing him first to the family and then to all the others.

Guests began to clap for silence so they could toast the reunion of the three Danes. The children were ecstatic. The party was complete.

✤ 14 ✤
The Mystery Unfolded

With all the toasts, the food, the singing and dancing, the added gaiety that Peter's arrival gave the party, there was no time to cross-examine him. But Karl *had* at least to find out how he had found him. He could wait for the rest.

As soon as there was a quiet moment, he asked.

Karl's persistence in his hunt for Peter had paid off. In the months that had elapsed since he first placed the notice for Peter in the Göteborg paper, its editor's services on behalf of refugees from Denmark had become famous throughout Sweden. When Peter finally reached Sweden, the first person he asked for help had directed him to the paper. As soon as he mentioned Karl's name, the editor pulled a letter out of his file and gave Peter his friend's address and phone number. The ad Karl had run so long and his letter discontinuing it had stuck in the editor's mind.

It was a simple, mischievous impulse that made Peter decide to come direct to Uppsala, without forewarning.

He explained: "I was so excited about getting here safely at last, it was as if I were drunk. All I could think of was seeing you. The idea of walking in like that and asking someone to pay the taxi—it made me laugh to myself. The luxury of having fun again! I couldn't resist."

Nor could Karl resist him. He had forgotten what Peter's good humor, his talent for practical jokes, could make of a perfectly ordinary day. It was like the icing on a plain sponge cake.

Where had he been? How did he get to Sweden? These questions were not answered until early Christmas morning. They were not even asked until well past midnight, after Father Christmas had paid his extended visit, the last of the guests' sleigh bells had tinkled off over the snow, and the children had tumbled wearily and happily upstairs and (with the help of Else, Karl, and Peter) into bed.

Then Peter began. He had been given his place in the line of refugees leaving the nurses' residence in Copenhagen the night Karl and Else left, but something went wrong. Just as he was about to leave—having counted slowly to a hundred after the man in front of him had set out, as he had been told to do—the nurse touched his shoulder and took him aside.

There had been a mistake. Their convoy was one too large. He was the last of the young people. The nurse had to sacrifice someone. She decided that he could stand the suspense of another wait better than the others.

She was probably right, Peter confessed. If he'd known what was ahead, he might have had the wit to be scared. But they'd done so well up till then that, except for his concern for Karl and Else, whom he knew would think he'd hit trouble, it never occurred to him to worry. He went back to the living room and the dog-eared magazines.

All that night, all the next day, he waited. Most of the time he was alone. The nurse went out. She came back at dusk the following evening and told him to go at once and catch a taxi that would pull up for him around the corner on the avenue bordering the canal. The driver would give him directions.

Everything went all right at first. He took a train going north. His first day was spent in the house of a minister—perhaps forty miles above and a bit west of Copenhagen. From there, dressed as a pastor, he bicycled with his host to a teacher's cottage fifteen miles beyond. He left there after dinner, having changed to sport jacket and slacks, with another man and two girls and took a second train north. They got off at Gilleleje and took the girls home.

During the evening at the teacher's, he had been alerted to the concern of the Resistance over the increasing evidence of *stikkers* in the neighborhood. Two Resistance workers had failed to report at the last rendezvous. But Peter still felt secure about his own chances. It was a complete surprise when, instead of being met by a new guide at the Gilleleje station, they were stopped by an armed agent of the Nazis.

They were taken to a temporary detention center and put under SS guard. In the next twenty-four hours, two more members of the Danish Resistance joined them. One of their new companions had been at the teacher's for dinner the preceding evening.

Three nights after their arrest, they were loaded onto a train full of prisoners, headed for Elsinore. They were well aware of what was ahead. Their Danish companions had told them they would be transferred to a prison ship and sent to Poland. That was all they needed to know. By that time there had been enough rumors and short-wave broadcasts about the Nazis' disposition of their political enemies to convince them that internment meant death—by starvation, from disease, or by some more exquisite form of torture.

Peter said that even then he was not really afraid. There wasn't time. He made a fast decision. He knew his only chance of survival was escape. He might be hurt getting off the train. He might be shot if discovered. He might be betrayed by one of his companions before he could get away. He might be recaptured. Nevertheless, there was no choice but to broach his plan and hope they'd come along. If he stayed on that train, he would never get out of German hands alive.

Peter, the two members of the Danish Resistance, and the other few who had been arrested with him were in the second compartment from the rear of the railroad car. There were two guards patrolling and an unknown number scattered in the compartments. Peter could not be certain that the so-called Danish underground members who had been put into his cell in the detention center were not really Nazi stool pigeons in disguise, even though he had met one at the teacher's.

The risk was there, but it had to be taken. The one danger he thought he could cope with was the patrolling guards. They started simultaneously from either end of the car and walked back and forth continuously. He would have to time his escape carefully.

He proposed his plan to the others soon after they left Gilleleje. They would jump out of the window and run for it. The other Jew and one of the Resistance men agreed. The last member of the foursome elected to stay behind. He thought there might be a better chance to escape later.

They waited until the train picked up speed after the next stop. They chose a moment when the guard had just passed their door. Then they dropped the windows and hurled themselves out blindly. The ground was soft. They were unhurt. By the time the train whistle began to screech insistently, they had gotten at least three hundred yards away from the tracks. Someone applied the air brakes. The train ground to a stop. Searchlights played on the surrounding moors. There was no place to hide, so they plunged blindly ahead, looking for safe cover. Bushes, trees, even long grass would be preferable to the wind-stunted heather they were going through.

Recounting the escape that night at the Holmgrens', Peter could give no rational explanation for their success, but they were successful. The searchlights continued to scan the fields. There was an occasional shot—perhaps some guard trying to prove his zeal. But they must have gotten beyond the range of the lights. In five minutes the sky was dark again. The train began to move once more.

The only worry was finding help. They were lucky again.

It was after midnight. There was little chance that anyone would be up in this rural area. So, when they came upon a lighted house, they took a chance. Would the inhabitants be friends? If they were friends—that is, loyal Danes—would they believe that their night visitors were really escaping the Nazis or suspect them of being *stikkers* looking for members of the Resistance?

They held their breaths and knocked. A woman opened the door. They explained their situation. She looked at them skeptically and started to retreat. There were sounds of a party behind her. The refugees kept trying to persuade her. When they had almost given up, her husband came to find out what was happening.

As soon as the Dane began to talk, the man flung open the door and asked them in. Addressing their spokesman, he offered any help he could. The Dane whom Peter had at one point suspected of being a spy was one of the most trusted Resistance workers in the area. Their host, who was the leader of the Resistance in the village, had worked with him and knew him well.

They spent the night tucked away in the attic. The next morning, outfitted in "new" clothes from the ward-

robe the leader's wife kept on hand for amateur theat-
ricals, they were transferred in a police van to the local
jail.

They were to stay there until a new convoy was
formed and then leave for Sweden. That very night
they were awakened and told to get ready. When Peter
tried to get up, he was stopped short by the leg pain he
knew so well. He did his best to conceal it, but it was
no use. The leap from the train must have activated the
old trouble. It was impossible to put his weight on that
leg. Once more he was left behind.

He never saw the others again. His Gilleleje host
wanted to send him back to the hospital in Copenhagen,
but too much had happened. The arrest and escape
were of course known throughout the Occupation's In-
telligence force. It would be foolhardy to expose himself. Anyway, as he explained to his protectors, there
was little that a hospital could do that couldn't be
done right where he was. Doctors knew no more about
how to cure his illness than they did about what had
caused it in the first place. The only treatment they
could prescribe was rest—complete rest.

Peter went back to the house on the moors where he
had first found refuge, and there he stayed, bedridden,
day after day, week after week, knowing that as long as
he remained, the leader, his wife, and his children, if
not the entire local Resistance movement, were endan-
gered.

Each morning he would try, gingerly, to stand, with
the same discouraging result. His right leg was like jelly
beneath him. When the pain finally subsided, he began

to be hopeful. Two weeks before he arrived in Uppsala, to the very day, he had been able to stand for the first time. Overjoyed at this sign that he was getting better, he wanted to walk, but his hostess forced him back to bed at once, fearful that he might undo the scant progress he had made.

For another ten days he kept to his room. Each morning he stood a little, then rested a little, then tried a step or two, until finally he could stand, walk, go up and down stairs—all without pain. Only then did they lay plans for his escape to Sweden. Extraordinary precautions had to be taken. It was clear Peter would not be able to climb, jump, run, or crawl—any or all of which might be necessary during an escape, as the situation in Denmark then stood.

Things in December were far different than they had been in early October. The Danish Resistance movement had anticipated the Nazi order to arrest the Jews well before it came through and had laid its plans carefully. There had been rumors for a year that the order would come, and with good reason. It was common knowledge that the Germans had imprisoned or exterminated the Jews in each successive country they had overrun. But there was an additional basis for the Danes' apparent foreknowledge of the exact date of the Nazis' October 1 decree. It was reliably reported that officials high in the Nazi Occupation government warned their Danish friends of what was coming.

When the decree was actually issued, the Danish response was automatic. Their plans to save the Jews went into effect at once. Before the decree, if any of the underground members were in danger, the Resistance had ways to speed them to safety in Sweden. The machinery worked smoothly and efficiently.

Now, the code words, the couriers, the drivers, the routes, the way stations, the boats, the policemen, the mailmen, the ministers and school teachers, the doctors and nurses, the fishermen and customs officers, the harbor police and Boy Scouts and bands of high-school boys wanting to be men, the sailors and taxi drivers, the ambulances, government launches, fishing boats, and delivery trucks were ready to perform the same service for the Jews. For this vast mission, the underground forces were augmented by an army of ordinary citizens, coming to the rescue of neighbors, friends, and relatives.

The Nazis had no preparation for their new program. They had been living for three years in a country that enjoyed favored status among Hitler's vassals. Denmark was respected if not pampered. King Christian was allowed the whimsical privilege of exercising his horse through the streets of the capital every morning, followed by a crowd of cheering subjects and his faithful bodyguard. The people were spared the guards, curfews, searches, and insults that would remind them of their captive state. Sometimes the Nazis, in their cringing efforts to be friendly, seemed more like vanquished than victors.

Thus, when Hitler changed his tune, the Occupation forces in Denmark, from the leadership down to the lowliest private, were taken by surprise. They needed a few days after the decree was issued to learn how to get tough, to adjust to the notion that there were Jewish villains among the pleasant Danes, who had to be removed. They needed time, too, for the mechanical readjustment—time to tighten up guard details, sharpen inspection, and strengthen small town patrols.

But if the Danes were ready, many Danish Jews were as surprised as the Nazis. After all, they had been Danes for centuries. They had never been segregated or separated from their non-Jewish fellow citizens. They had never been identified by registration. They had intermarried, in many cases, generation after generation. Hitler could not mean them. It was not real. They could not believe the order. They had to see a sister, whose husband was not Jewish even by ancestry, arrested. They had to hear about friends disappearing in the night before they would leave. Then they left in panic, and it was at this point that the orderly, unobtrusive, systematic underground railroad of the Resistance, which had quietly shepherded thousands to safety, began to break down.

By the time Peter was able to leave, the risk of capture had increased immeasurably. The weather on Öresund—the water between Denmark and Sweden—was another obstacle.

The last days, while he waited for plans to be completed and prayed that his leg would not act up again, at least until he was out of Denmark, were the worst. Faithfully he exercised, just enough to keep his strength without risking any strain on the vulnerable right side.

The actual flight, when it came, was anticlimactic. He was awakened in the middle of the night. The Re-

sistance leader handed him a uniform and cap and told
him to put it on and come downstairs. Five minutes
later, in the well-tailored uniform of a Danish Customs
inspector, he followed his host over the moor to the road.
In a matter of seconds a police car stopped, his friend
shook hands and wished him luck, and he got in beside
the driver. In a quarter of an hour he was on board a
government Customs launch, speeding out to sea. His
superior officer told him they were headed due east for
Hälsingborg in Sweden. His duties were explained. He
was the relief officer. He could retire to the small cabin
below until called.

The boat was stopped twice. Peter heard fragments
of routine interrogation from what seemed to be German patrols. Then the permission to proceed was given.
They went on.

About an hour after they started, the Customs inspector came below and prepared him for the next move.
They were approaching a Swedish fishing vessel they
knew. They would order him to stop. While the Customs men were going over the Swedish boat, Peter was
to slip into the cabin, where he would find fishermen's
clothes to change to. He would give the uniform he was
wearing to one of the Danish sailors and remain behind on the Swedish vessel.

Everything went smoothly. The fishing boat was tiny.
The captain and one sailor were its full complement.
They were obviously veterans—both as fishermen and
ferrymen to freedom.

Peter stepped ashore before dawn. He had identifying
papers, full directions about where to go for help, money

to see him through, and warm clothes. It was all he could do to get his rescuers to wait long enough to be thanked. They were in great haste to be off. He suspected there was a second rendezvous scheduled before daylight.

✳ 15 ✳
Planning for Peace

Right after Christmas Peter started talking about looking for a job. When the Holmgrens told him that no one in Sweden thinks about business between Christmas and New Year's, he agreed to relax until after the holidays. During the next week, everyone concentrated on persuading him not to look at all.

Mr. Holmgren told him he'd have little chance of getting farm work until spring. Mrs. Holmgren wanted him to take care of his health. She pointed out that the carrying and lifting and riding in rough farm vehicles would be the worst possible medicine for his ailing leg. Finally he yielded to her pleading that he go back to Stockholm with Else and consult an orthopedist before trying to find a job.

He came back to the farm a few days later, considerably chastened. Doctors have a habit of issuing orders first and thinking about how they can be carried out later. The specialist Peter went to examined him and took X-rays. His verdict: "You have no business standing up, let alone wandering all over Europe."

Peter protested that he had not had much choice. It made no impression. The doctor said with quiet finality: "That may have been so. But you have a choice now. You go back where you came from near Uppsala and don't stir from that house for three months."

Peter explained that he had no money for rent, and the doctor said flatly: "You'll make out, I'm sure. There is a train leaving this afternoon. See that you take it. Come back in April."

In a way, the doctor's orders proved a blessing in disguise. They opened a new life to Peter. He felt he could not possibly "live off" the Holmgrens. While he spent a lot of time talking with the children—stimulating their curiosity for study, reading to them, telling them stories, helping them with lessons, teaching the older ones Latin and chess—he considered that fun. He would never put a price tag on it, though Mr. Holmgren tried to convince him that it was valuable to him. In his view there was only one way he could earn his keep— by helping Karl.

He suggested that he could draw up plans for the furniture Karl was commissioned to make, detail the specifications, and estimate the cost of materials and time required. As a result Karl was able to give his customers much more reliable estimates in advance and insure himself a much better rate of profit. In addition, Peter's contribution allowed Karl more time to turn out the work.

By the time Peter paid a second visit to the orthopedist, the boys' business had almost doubled. Peter was
at last ready to admit that he was pulling his share of
the load at the Holmgrens'. He was not only doing
paper work but also helping with turning, carving,
sanding, and other details of finishing. When the doctor told him that he could never expect to go back to
farming, he was not disappointed. He was not a farmer
at heart, and as long as he could contribute equally to
his partnership with Karl, he was content. At least he
was no longer required to keep to the house. He could
walk—as long as he avoided strenuous climbing. He
could ride a bicycle—as long as he was sensible about
not overdoing it. More important, he could work standing up. In short, he was freer to enjoy life and help Karl.

The boys worked together in Uppsala for over a year.
Before the end of 1944, their business had outgrown the
space in the barn that Mr. Holmgren could spare. They
built a new workshop next door to give them the extra
room they needed.

They made occasional trips to Stockholm to visit
Else or the orthopedist, to investigate some rumor that
had trickled through about one of their relatives. But
their lives had become firmly rooted in the town where
they were almost as well known now as the Holmgrens,
whose families had been there for centuries. So, when
they told Mr. Holmgren, a few days after news of the
Nazi surrender was broadcast in May, 1945, that they
must make plans to return to Denmark, he was as
shocked as if his eldest son had announced that he would
not live on the farm.

"Haven't you been happy here?" he asked sadly. "Can't we get you some land for yourselves?"

They tried to explain that, in spite of their devotion to the family, Denmark was home to them.

"But why not adopt Sweden instead?" he suggested.

Neither of the boys turned down the suggestion. They temporarily postponed plans to leave. The chairman of the municipal council of their village came to the farm. After lunch he asked the boys to join him in Mr. Holmgren's study and invited them, formally, to become citizens of the country where they had made such a useful place for themselves.

It was time to speak. Karl began: "We want you to understand that even though our gratitude and affection for all of you is too great to express, we are Danish and want to go home."

The man looked surprised. "But aren't you Germans?"

Peter answered: "We *were* German. If we had remained Germans, where would we be today? Denmark is where we first found freedom. It is a motherland to us."

Karl broke in. "Perhaps we have been luckier than most people our age. What happened to us is not recommended. But it may have had some advantages. We learned how evil men can be when we were still children. Since then, we have found out how good they can be. I don't think we'll ever forget."

"Of course not, and we'll be back. We'll show you that it doesn't take any longer to get to Uppsala from Denmark in peacetime than it does when you're fleeing for your life," Peter added.

In the next few days the family tried to reconcile themselves to losing Karl and Peter. Else had given up her position and come for a last visit. The night before all three were to leave, the Holmgrens gave a farewell party that outdid even the Christmas Eve dinner.

A few days later the three refugees were back home in Copenhagen again. They found themselves the simplest and cheapest rooms they could. Else began to look for work, and the boys started going through the red tape that would open the way to citizenship. A foreigner must live in Denmark ten years before he can apply for citizenship. But one must work to live, and to get a job, a foreigner must get a work permit. That was the first order of business.

It seemed that Denmark was as uninterested in having them for adopted sons as Sweden had been eager. When Karl first went to the immigration office, he was told to return the following week, after they'd had time to look up his records.

At the next visit he was referred to a senior officer. He waited in the man's outer office for an intolerable length of time. At last a rejected suppliant came out and asked the receptionist where she could appeal. On this pessimistic note, Karl went in for his interview.

"Tell me, young man," the officer began without looking up from the papers on his desk, "how do you expect a little country like Denmark to support every foreigner who chooses to work here? Who knows that you could *find* a job? You have no employment record.

As far as I can see, you never even finished trade school."

Karl tried not to notice the man's discouraging attitude. "But sir," he said, "I supported myself during the war. I am a skilled cabinetmaker. You can see my record from Sweden. If I could manage then, I certainly can get along now."

This time the officer looked up. "But you are a German. Men like you are needed to rebuild your country."

At this Karl forgot his mission and spoke impulsively, devil take the consequences. "I don't think so. There is nothing of me, nothing of mine, there. Germany gave me nothing and took everything. Germany does not need me."

The man was looking down at the papers again. As if to himself, he read: "Mother's whereabouts—unknown. Father's whereabouts—unknown. Relatives—unknown."

Then he looked at Karl. "Have you satisfied yourself that further inquiries are futile?"

Slowly Karl said: "If you would suggest?"

"I see you have contacted the Red Cross, the Jewish organizations, the International Refugee organizations, the officials in Düsseldorf—without success."

Karl nodded.

"Give me a week, then come back." He stood up to end the interview.

Peter had about the same experience with his application.

It was a tense period. Without work permits they were not allowed to take permanent jobs. There was nothing to do but wait and hope that their savings would last. The one thing they wanted to avoid was having to ask the Troners in Fynshav for help.

They had decided not to get in touch with them until their applications had been granted and they had found work. They dreamed of going with presents for everyone to take the family by surprise. When they realized that it might be weeks longer before they were settled, they changed their plans. That was too long to postpone a reunion with the closest thing to a family either of them had left.

They left Copenhagen with Else the morning after Karl's frustrating second visit to the immigration office. Back-tracking over the route they had come a year and a half before was quite a different experience.

In Denmark, spring comes gently. The scattered trees that in July would be a sturdy forest green now showed the barest feathering of delicate gold-chartreuse. The fields were gently colored, too, with freshly sprouting grains and grasses, and the sky was a changeable thing. Fresh gusts blew clouds of down across it. The days could change from sun to shower in minutes.

To stretch their precious savings, they hitchhiked, taking any ride they could get—horse, truck, or car. Their spirits had begun to lift at the mere prospect of seeing their friends. They were so gay that Else told them they acted as if their citizenship was already in the bag.

A few minutes before they reached Korsør, they got caught in a shower and fought over which one should yield his jacket to keep Else dry. When she suggested taking shelter, they called her a granny.

"Afraid of a little rain," Peter teased. When the shower was over, they took off their shirts, wrung them out, and put them back on to dry, and dry they did in the wind. By the time they had reached the ferry to Nyborg, there was no sign that they had ever been rained on at all.

Once aboard, they went straight to the dining room, but while they ordered food for Else, they would take nothing but beer themselves.

"If we ate," Peter explained seriously, "we wouldn't feel the beer. That would be a waste of beer, and we can't afford to be extravagant."

They got to Fynshav at dusk, almost the exact hour they had left. The streets were practically empty. The few people they saw didn't know them. When they reached the entrance to the school, they felt suddenly awkward and stopped to debate whether they should go in without knocking.

"Maybe we'd better not," Karl said. "The Troners may not even be here any more."

That was such an unthinkable prospect that they knocked and rang both and could hardly bear the wait until someone came. The someone was a young lady. When Karl asked for Mr. Troner, she said he was at dinner and added: "May I tell him who's calling?"

It was the oldest Troner child. The boys recognized her voice, but they gave their names with straight faces, waiting for the reaction. Now the young lady became a child again. With a leap of joy she was in Peter's arms, then in Karl's, with what seemed a single movement. Then, without a word, she was off through the family apartment to the school dining room to spread the news. Karl, Peter, and Else followed her, arriving at the entrance to the dining room just as she had delivered their message. The whole family was standing up. A hush fell over the room as the students recognized something unusual was taking place. Tim broke the silence, shouting: "Karl!"

In a second he was on top of his old friend—literally —for the "little boy" now towered over the older one. Karl, though full-grown, was only of average height. Tim was going to be a giant. His neck was long and thin. His hands and feet were so big and awkward you could tell that he was going to have to grow even taller before he learned to adjust to the shape of the man he would be.

Before five minutes had passed, it seemed to the boys that they had never been away. The children had grown. Mr. Troner had some gray hair in his sideburns. Mrs. Troner was wearing a new sweater. Everything else was unchanged.

The next day Karl had time for a sail with Tim in a new sloop his father had given him. Else had time to get acquainted with Mrs. Troner and the girls, and Peter had time to visit the Larsens on the farm.

In the evening, after dinner, Mr. Troner asked the boys to have coffee with him alone in his study. It gave them a chance to talk over their plans for the future. He urged them to go on with their studies. But even when he offered to help them get fellowships, they were unwilling.

Karl was in too much of a hurry. "I've lost so much

time already," he said. "I want to be able to earn my way and get settled in life."

Peter's objection was a little different. "Maybe later," was his response. "But now I feel the way Karl does. I can't accept any more help. I want to be on my own."

Mr. Troner gave up trying to persuade them. "Maybe Tim will change your minds," he said, joking. "I want to send him to Copenhagen to school next fall to prepare for the university."

"He'll live with me, won't he?" Karl asked.

"I can't see him doing anything else, can you?" The headmaster and Karl smiled.

The next morning Mrs. Troner loaded the three wanderers with enough food to keep them for weeks. Then they were driven to the shore, where they stowed their gear in Tim's new Lightning and jumped in after it to sail for the ferry in Mommark.

This time there was no need to beach the boat in a hidden cove. They slid right up to the dock next to the ferry. Lugging their sacks and duffel, Peter and Karl jumped ashore and helped Else. Then, waving good-by, they raced to get on before the gangplank was lifted. Tim had already pushed off smartly on a starboard tack, heading up to Fynshav.

Back in Copenhagen, three days later, Peter and Karl both received telegrams summoning them to the immigration office at the same hour. The man who had offered so little encouragement the week before now stood up, extending his hand to each of them in turn. "We've satisfied ourselves that Denmark needs you," he said, skipping preliminaries. "Your applications have been granted." They shook hands again, thanked him, and prepared to leave. He detained them. "We have received a specific grant that will allow you to reestablish your partnership in the cabinet-making business here."

When they asked him to explain, he was mysterious. "I'm not at liberty to name the donor. Generous people, as you know, often dislike having others beholden to them. But there *was* a suggestion accompanying the gift. Shall I read it?"

The boys nodded. "These are boys who will use this help well. If they are ever in a position to give the same kind of support to others, they will offer it without being asked."

It was a graceful compliment, and a touching one. The officer looked at them, pleased.

They thanked him again. Peter said: "I hope you'll assure our benefactors that we shall not disappoint them."

They said good-by. Now they were settled at last. Else, who wanted to become a teacher, had been given a job in a kindergarten. In return for serving as an assistant, she would get room, board, and tuition at a training school for nursery-school teachers.

They felt so sure of their futures that they went out to dinner in a restaurant together and ordered wine to celebrate. Over the meal they tried to solve the mystery of their benefactor. Was it the Troners? The Holmgrens? Else's Stockholm family? Or perhaps that cool immigration officer himself? The Nordbys in Jutland, the Larsens, the gentle widow Karl lived with when he first came to Denmark?

Suddenly they were struck with the magnitude of their good fortune. Else hated to see them get solemn. There had been enough of that. As a Dane, it was her privilege to make light of her countrymen's nobility. "Don't get all choked up over us Danes. We only do what any decent human being would do for another."

In the years to come, that modest explanation would be offered again and again by Danes to minimize their rescue of their Jewish countrymen.

"Come on," Else urged them. "Let's have fun tonight. We'll go to Tivoli and dance. It won't cost much."

They had started on the long road to citizenship. In ten years they would be allowed to petition Parliament to declare them Danes by vote. The next day their names appeared in a news item about refugees who had been given work permits. Karl cut the article out of the newspaper, for some sentimental reason, and put it aside to keep.

Two evenings later, when he came home from looking for a new workshop with Peter, he found a letter under his door. It was addressed in German script and postmarked Copenhagen.

"Dear Sir," it began. "I was in Auschwitz concentration camp with your mother. When she was very ill, she asked me to take this and give it to you if I ever found you. I saw your name in the paper today. She asked me to send you her love and tell you that there is no one left."

Karl held in his hand the soiled yellow star of David with "JUDE" etched on it in black, the emblem of the Nazi victim, the "dog tag" of the Jew: all that remained of his father, the stern and just, his mother whose comfort never failed him, his brother whom he dreamed of bringing to safety.

The tears he had never allowed to flow came unbidden and unchecked. When they were all gone, he put the star carefully back into the envelope with the note and slid it under the paper that lined his drawer, where it would be safe. He soaked his face in icy water until he could breathe properly again, washed, changed his shirt, combed his hair carefully, and left his room. He was going to find Else. He did not want to be alone any more.